HEA

WAITING

ROOM

By

CLARE WILSON

Published by Clare Wilson

First print: January 2014
First ebook: January 2014

Copyright © 2010 by Clare Wilson
All rights reserved.

All comment and pictures are attributed solely to the author. No part of this book may be used or reproduced in any manner whatsoever without written permission, except in the case of brief quotations embodied in critical articles and reviews.

To contact the author email:
havenshawmanor@gmail.com

Facebook: *www.facebook.com/clare.wilson.1422*

Twitter: *@staffwielder*

Cover Design & Artwork: Paul Gildea

ISBN: 13: 978-1495212093

DEDICATION: *This book is dedicated to all those searching to find where they truly belong. Sometimes, you don't need to look as far as you think...*

ACKNOWLEDGEMENTS: *There are a lot of people I have to thank for this story. Firstly, I'd like to thank my long suffering husband for being so patient with me. I'd also like to thank my mum and my dear friend Becky for giving the book a thorough once over. Finally, I'd like to thank one Mr Paul Gildea. Not only is he a loyal friend, but he has given me un-wavering support, and even more amazing artwork, over the past few years.*

Chapter One
Realisation

I don't know exactly when it happened. I think it took me a little time to realise what was going on. I wasn't used to getting a great deal of attention at home, so things seemed pretty normal at first. I sat on a bench in the kitchen watching my sister make breakfast. A pop tart in the toaster, she bobbed about to the music coming out of the earphones which seemed to be permanently attached to her head these days. We hadn't actually spoken to one another in some time. Since mum had gone, none of us had a lot to say to each other. She'd taken the life out of the place with her when she left, literally.

Time was passing very strangely. I couldn't remember the previous evening and outside it was starting to look like autumn. The morning was slightly too dark for summer, the golden leaves being whipped from the trees by the blustering wind. Summer seemed to have passed me by completely. I made a mental note, *get out more.*

Since mum had gone, nothing seemed to work normally around here. My sister didn't seem to see it, but the house was dead. Dad spent as little time as possible at home and I had become a hermit since finishing school. He didn't seem to notice that I hadn't done anything about university. I knew this was strange, but decided that if I kept my head down, it would buy me some time. I had no idea what I wanted to do. I had told him I was going to take a gap year, but he hadn't actually agreed. He didn't say a lot to me these days. In fact, I couldn't actually remember the last time he had spoken to me. I was taking his silence as a form of agreement.

It was on this dreary grey morning that I noticed *her*. She was watching me intently from the kitchen window waving her hand periodically, eagerly trying to get my attention.

I meandered out into the garden; the walk made me feel rather light headed. I would need to eat something when I got inside. 'Can I help you?' I asked, trying to sound short. I had learned that in London, you didn't encourage strangers. It was just the way things were done. Everyone survived by being mutually rude to one another. It seemed to work in a bizarre way.

She looked relieved that I had noticed her. 'Thank God,' she said, sighing. 'I was considering giving up. Not the most perceptive are you?'

'Who are you?' I asked, feeling irritation rise in me at her words. I wasn't in the mood for some odd-ball insulting me.

'Who I am isn't important,' she said, standing up properly and straightening her dress. It was then that I noticed how she looked. I had only been able to see her head from my position in the kitchen. She wore a fitted floor length gown which brushed along the ground as she walked towards me. Each step had a silent elegance. I had never seen anyone quite like her.

'Do you mind telling me what's going on?' I asked. 'What's with the Halloween costume?' I continued, motioning to her strange outfit. While I was trying to sound nonchalant, I couldn't hide my awe at her appearance.

'I'm not sure what you mean,' she said, holding her head up proudly. 'Portia, I'm here to help you.'

'How do you know my name?' I was light-headed once more, the whole thing was making me feel decidedly uneasy. It must be hunger, surely it must be hunger. I couldn't remember my last meal after all.

'I'm just like you,' she said, smiling. 'If you trust me, I can help you. There's no need for you to be afraid.'

'I don't understand...' I muttered, looking around the garden, confused.

'I see,' she said. Something about her face showed that my words had given her cause for concern. 'May I?' she asked, gesturing towards the door.

'Of course,' I replied, still completely confused by this strange turn of events. I had no idea why I was inviting this odd woman into our home, we'd barely met. I shook my head and turned back towards the house.

She followed me inside. I noticed that my sister had gone and the house felt even emptier than it had before. No-one was there. I didn't know how exactly I knew no-one was home, I just knew.

'Take a seat,' she said, motioning towards the bench.

I sat down blindly. It was odd. I had a feeling that I already knew what she was going to say and who she was, although I couldn't seem find the words. It was like struggling to remember a long forgotten dream. I could remember the feel of the dream, just not what it was actually about.

'My name is Mary,' she said, smiling at me kindly.

Her voice was strange, gentle and well-spoken. She definitely didn't come from the local estate. She sounded like someone from a period drama on the television, a first class passenger from the Titanic.

'Were you in the shed?' I asked. It seemed mundane, but somehow the woman looked dusty, grey. Even in my strange state of confusion, my brain wanted at least one part of this encounter to make sense.

'No,' she replied, laughing lightly and touching her hair.

'What's so funny?' I asked, wondering when these questions would stop. I had never asked so many questions in my life. I wasn't really the type. Things usually just happened around me.

'When was the last time you looked in a mirror?' she enquired, still giggling but trying to hide it.

'I don't do that very often,' I mumbled. 'Not since…'

'Yes?' she asked.

'Not since my mum left,' I barked, I hated saying the words aloud. 'After she went, my dad used to look at pictures of us both, he used to rant that we looked so alike. It was as though there was something wrong with me. I guess I just stopped looking, it was easier that way.'

Mary placed a hand on my shoulder. 'Well, perhaps it's time. I think you need to look at yourself. I'll be with you, it won't be so hard.'

I nodded, stood up and walked into the living room, stopping in front of the large mirror above the fire place. Mary seemed to come with me, her movements almost fluid. I didn't know why I was doing what this woman asked of me, but it just seemed natural; the first natural thing I had felt for ages. After a few seconds, I looked up and a gasp escaped my lips.

She smiled. 'You see?' she asked.

'I don't know,' I muttered. Deep down, I knew that was a lie. I think some part of me had known what I was going to see before I looked in the mirror.

'I think you do, Portia,' she said, smiling gently.

'So I'm…' I whispered, unable to get the words out.

'Yes,' she said.

'When?' I asked.

'Some time ago,' she said, shrugging her shoulders. 'Time isn't so important when you're like us.'

'Time,' I muttered, parroting everything she was saying to me. 'What now?'

'Well,' she said in a measured way, examining her reflection in a very feminine manner. 'I'll show you the ropes and then you can decide where you want to be.'

'That sounds like a bit of an anti-climax,' I replied, turning to face her. 'Shouldn't there be more than this?'

'What do you mean, dear?' she asked, reaching out to fix a hair which had fallen into my eyes. She didn't look much older than me, but she spoke to me as though I was a mere child. In many ways I felt like one. She seemed so self-assured, confident.

'What do I mean?' I spluttered, feeling my frustration rising once more. 'I mean, I've seen the movies, there's supposed to be more than this, an angel on a cloud or my grandmother waiting to guide me into a bright light!'

Mary smiled. Her face was rather beautiful. If you looked closely, beyond her grey paleness, she had piercing green eyes and perfect porcelain features. Her hair must have been baby blonde at one time. 'No-one knows what happens until they get here,' she said. 'I can explain the rules, as far as I know them.'

'The rules?' I asked, angry tears welling up in my eyes, despite Mary's efforts to be gentle. 'I don't want to learn the rules. I'm dead!'

As far as I was aware, we had walked into the kitchen. However, yet again, time seemed to have shifted before me. It was dark outside, and I could hear my sister upstairs pottering around in her room.

'So what are these rules?' I asked shakily, walking over to turn the kettle on. If in doubt, a cup of tea always helped things, or made you feel as if it were helping things. I stopped in my tracks. 'Not necessary?' I asked.

'No,' she said, sitting down by the table, 'not at all. I'm not saying you can't turn it on, just that it won't be a lot of use to you once it's boiled.'

I still couldn't take this in. Even though it felt like giving in to an inevitable truth I had already known, there was still something too final about the whole thing. 'Do you know what happened to me?' I asked.

'Not really,' she said, 'you'll be the only one who can figure that out. I wouldn't get too hung up on that point; some of us never remember exactly what happened.'

'Right,' I muttered. 'So how did you know I was here?'

'I just sensed you,' she said, thoughtfully. 'Once you're more used to this you'll start to know what I mean, although, I have a gift. I can feel people who need help. I know when someone is lost. Once you're experienced, you'll be able to sense a little flickering spark in your peripheral vision. With me it's more detailed than that. If someone is lost, I can see their face; know their name and where they are. I noticed you and I wanted to come and help. It's become a bit of a duty for me; the others are pretty used to it by now.'

'Others?' I asked.

'Yes,' Mary said, 'I *stay* I imagine is the right word, with some other people.'

'Right,' I said, almost to myself. 'You live with some people. So there's no tunnel into a bright light?' I asked, leaning back against the worktop and feeling my hands sink into it a few inches before I stopped them. I tried to ignore the strange sensation. I wanted to hear what Mary was going to say.

'No,' she said. 'Well, that's not strictly true. Suffice to say, there is no tunnel for us. This is where we belong.'

'I wasn't a bad person,' I muttered, wondering why I wouldn't get the full experience. 'I thought that…' I trailed off.

'Of course not,' she said standing up and crossing the room towards me. 'Think about this logically. How many people have ever lived upon the earth?'

'I don't know,' I mused, puzzled by such a question. 'I wouldn't have thought that would have mattered a great deal. Isn't Heaven supposed to be this all expansive place of peace and rest? That's what they taught us at Sunday school. No-one ever mentioned that there were issues with the population per square mile.'

'Well,' she sighed, 'I'm afraid what you were taught doesn't really matter. That was all people just trying to hazard a guess. They couldn't actually know what goes on. As I said, no-one does until they get here. I'll try to keep this as simple as I can. There have always been those who chose to stay here, people who wouldn't leave loved ones, or perhaps had unfinished business. Even those who, for fear of retribution, would refuse to pass over. However, now it's more a case of numbers. Heaven can only hold a limited number of souls. After a while, the powers that be decided to put stricter entry requirements in place.'

'Right,' I said, trying to take in what she was telling me.

'So what the church says is wrong?' I asked. I had never been a devoted believer, but I liked the fundamentals, you know, if you live a good life, God will take care of you. Eternal peace in exchange for enduring everything you suffer while on earth. I couldn't see that I had deviated from that particularly. In fact, considering my years, I felt I had suffered more than most.

'No,' she replied, tilting her head to one side and screwing up her nose. 'What Jesus came to say to us still holds true. It's just that in his day, there was plenty of room. He thought he could save all of mankind. He wasn't to know that the population would explode.'

'Okay,' I said, trying to make sense of what she was telling me.

'Basically,' she continued, 'under the current system, you need to be important to get in. Unfortunately we're not important enough. If you had been, you wouldn't be here.' She motioned to the room around her.

'You're telling me that only VIPs get into heaven?' I asked, feeling as if I was back at school all over again. Once more, I hadn't been picked for the netball team, how very typical.

'It's not about wealth or prestige, although sometimes the most important people tend to have money. It's more about what you've done with your life. In our situation, the most important people can often be the most humble. They try to be as fair as possible. I think children are allowed in without question.'

'I'm only eighteen,' I said, feeling bitter. 'I didn't exactly have a chance to make my mark on the world, to prove myself worthy. This is like going for a job interview without any experience. You won't get experience until someone takes a chance on you. It's not fair.'

'Such is death,' she said, smiling to herself. 'I too was taken from the world too young, and so, here we are. In fact, you've been rather unlucky. It depends on your time period etcetera, but if you are deemed to be a minor in your society, you tend to get in. If you had only passed before your eighteenth birthday, they might have considered your case.'

'That's a comforting thought,' I muttered, sighing. 'I missed out on my own afterlife because of a few weeks.' At least, I thought it was only a few weeks. I could definitely remember my birthday.

Mary shrugged. 'As I said, such is death.'

I shook my head. If she was going to start using cliché phrases adapted in that way, it was going to get very irritating, very fast. 'So, what are these rules?' I asked.

'They're pretty simple,' she replied, looking pleased that I had accepted her explanation. 'You need to ground yourself. You'll have noticed that time seems to shift. If you like to be around loved ones for birthdays or special occasions, you need to focus upon them. It's not too hard once you get the hang of it, and after a few decades, it isn't particularly important anyway.'

'That shouldn't really matter for me,' I said, 'decades or not. It doesn't seem as though they've noticed I'm gone. I don't think I'll feel guilty for not watching them blow out candles on a cake.'

'I doubt that,' Mary said, touching my shoulder for a moment. 'In fact, from what I have observed, I think that the emptiness in the house is because you're gone.'

I snorted, but liked the thought that perhaps they were missing me. 'It's not me that they're missing, it's my mum.'

'Is she one of us?' Mary asked.

'Not as far as I'm aware,' I mused, finding it strange that I no longer counted as being part of the normal world. 'She just left.'

'The next thing,' Mary said, glossing over the pain in my voice, 'is that you need to let go of the rules you were used to following with regard to doors and things.'

'What?' I asked.

'Well,' she said, 'while I still prefer to walk through doorways and sit upon furniture, it isn't strictly necessary. For me it's more about manners and decorum. It's most unseemly to stick your head through someone's wall and spy on them. If you want to be somewhere, you simply need to think about it, and you'll be there. Here,' she said, holding out her hand, 'I'll show you.'

I tentatively took it. I think I expected it to feel cold, but it didn't. It didn't feel warm particularly, but I liked the sensation.

Suddenly I noticed we were no longer in the kitchen.

With a start, I realised we were standing outside Buckingham Palace. 'Bloody hell,' I muttered.

'Really!' Mary tittered, obviously offended by my language.

'Sorry,' I said, unsure why I was apologising to this woman I had only met.

'Right,' she continued, 'you get the point. Anywhere you want to go, think of it, and hey presto!'

'Well,' I said, still completely in shock, 'I suppose it beats piling onto the tube.'

'The what?' she asked.

'Nothing,' I muttered.

She let go of my hand and before I knew it, we were standing back in my kitchen.

'It can also be useful for other things,' she said.

I didn't know whether she understood how freaked out I was, but she seemed to be determined to keep going. 'Like what?' I asked.

'Well,' she said, reaching out for my hand once more, 'it's probably easier if I show you.'

I tentatively took her hand, wondering where on earth we were going to end up next. The Taj Mahal?

As the room disappeared and I took in our new surroundings, I saw that we were standing in the midst of a busy hall which looked to be in a large manor house of some kind. There were crowds of people bustling around us, and it looked as if servants were preparing a feast. Great fires were lit and many places were set around rows of grand tables laid with stiff white table cloths.

'Where is this place?' I asked, unable to conceal my look of wonder. The whole scene was beautiful, a stately home, abuzz with life and warmth.

'This is my home,' Mary said, smiling at my reaction. 'It's the night before Christmas.'

'Wait a minute,' I said, taking in the style of dress of those around us. 'Does this mean we can travel through time?'

'Sort of,' she said, wrinkling her perfect little nose. 'It's not really time travel. It's going back to something which exists in your memory. It can be a nice experience when you're feeling low. A little perk they gave us after entry requirements changed, I understand. You don't need such a skill in Heaven, you see. Or rather, I'm led to believe. We don't really communicate with people who've crossed over. Our knowledge of what goes on is more hearsay than anything else.'

'Right,' I muttered.

'That's my father over there,' she said, distracted from her train of thought and pointing to a jolly man who was overseeing the proceedings. He was wearing a black evening jacket and crisp white shirt and tie. His extravagantly groomed moustache curled up at the edges and sat beneath his rosy cheeks. 'He loved to surprise me. This is the year when he had a new pony waiting for me out in the stables. I was ten.'

'I have a question,' I said. I didn't want to interrupt her, but there were so many things I needed to know.

'Another?' she mused, smiling. 'Forgive me. I know you must have many questions.'

'Yes,' I answered, smiling back at her. It was difficult not to feel happy in such surroundings. The whole scene emanated bliss. I wondered whether that was because we were feeling as Mary had felt at the time. 'If you can do this and all your family are obviously passed, do you *live* with them?'

'I don't,' she said sadly. 'Some do, but unfortunately I've never been able to find mine in this life. I like to think they were chosen to move on.' A deep sadness washed over her face. 'I told you I have a gift, I've spent a great deal of my time trying to use it to locate any of members of my family. Alas, they elude me. It's almost as if I can sense complete strangers, but I have a blind spot for the people I loved. As I said, perhaps the reason I cannot see them is because they're not here.'

She let go of my hand and suddenly we were back in my kitchen. When I looked round, I noticed that she was hiding her face.

'Any more rules I need to remember?' I asked, trying to change the subject. My previous question obviously seemed to have upset her.

This seemed to distract her from her melancholy. 'Well, you shouldn't really try to communicate with people who still live in this world.'

'No haunting,' I said, making a mental note.

'It's not polite,' she continued, qualifying her statement. 'There are plenty of people who do it, but it's not socially acceptable behaviour. More importantly, it's not a great deal of use anyway. It rarely works, and even when it does, all they feel is a cold breeze or an eerie feeling. From what I have been told, it can be incredibly frustrating. There are those who are more gifted at such things, but they're not the kind of people you want to have as acquaintances.'

'Right,' I said, nodding.

'Also,' she said, as though she had just remembered something, 'on that subject, there are certain spirits you would do best to avoid.'

I simply looked at her blankly.

'You'll know them when you see them,' she said, sensing my confusion. 'It's always obvious when they come along. They're the ones who stayed through fear, generally evil people. They like to prey upon the more vulnerable among us, so it's best to be careful.'

'It's not really fair to still have them here, when the people in charge expect us to live here now too,' I said, worrying about what would happen if I didn't know the bad from the good.

'Unfortunately there isn't a great deal of choice,' she said, smiling kindly. 'They don't really have a great deal of control down here. I believe it's linked to the whole free will thing. If someone has chosen to stay here, they can't force them to leave.'

'So why don't all bad people just stay here?' I asked, imagining this new world being full of evil spirits.

'I think that most people, either very good or very bad, pass over rather quickly. It's what they're supposed to do. I don't think it would be an easy compulsion to ignore. Those who do must have to really fight it.'

'So the place isn't full of evil ghosts?' I asked; her explanation hadn't made me feel a whole lot better.

'It's not so different from when you were alive,' she said. 'There will always be bad people in the world, Portia. Still, you should have an in-built sense of right and wrong, this will allow you to tell the good from the bad. Trust your instincts; it's what they're there for. Sometimes evil comes in attractive packages.'

'Like you?' I asked, now feeling slightly paranoid.

'No,' she said, rather insulted. 'Not like me. I'm merely here to help you. The bad ones have a different presence, it's like a smell or a taste, it's hard to describe. You'll know it if you see it. If you're ever unsure, just think of home and you'll be back here. They can't follow you somewhere like this, not unless you invite them in. We do have certain protections.'

'Right,' I said, nodding again. 'Is there anything else?'

'Not that I can think of right now,' she said, touching her chin demurely. 'You'll learn more of the finer details as you go. I can always come back and visit you if you like?'

'Oh,' I said. While she had been an unexpected visitor, I hadn't realised she was going to leave me so soon. I had no idea what I was doing. 'Do you need to leave?' I asked, probably sounding rather pathetic.

She reached out a hand and touched mine once more. 'I do, I'm sorry. I have people waiting for me. My husband will be wondering where I've gotten to. He doesn't like it when I'm away from his side for too long, it's sweet really.'

'Your husband?' I asked, confused since she had mentioned earlier that she had been unable to find any of her family in this life.

'He's my husband here,' she said, trying to explain. 'Obviously we haven't been legally married, but we have bound ourselves to one another as much as is possible in this place. We all form our own lives on this side. Some choose to live in isolation, but I was always used to having a family around me. While it isn't the family I was born to, we have been together so long I don't think I could live without them. Henry is wonderful. I don't think my life here would be so bearable if I didn't have him.'

I felt sad. How would I find my way with no-one to help me? I had never been very good at making friends. 'Can I come with you?' I asked.

'I don't know,' she replied. 'You shouldn't really be dragged from your old family so quickly, their presence can be a great help in the transition.'

'Okay,' I said, feeling bitterly disappointed. I couldn't see this house holding much comfort at the moment. It was as still as the grave.

She saw the look on my face. 'If you need me, all you have to do is call and I'll be here.'

'What's your number?' I asked out of habit, I felt like an idiot as soon as the words had crossed my lips.

She giggled. 'We don't use your modern gadgets, no need. If you simply call my name, I'll come.'

'Thanks,' I said, trying my best to smile. The prospect of her leaving me made me realise how lonely I had been over the past few months. Even though I had no proper sense of time passing, it had been hard. It now made sense why none of my old school friends had been in touch. They had known I had departed this world before I did; typical. 'What do I do now?' I asked.

'Explore,' she said, shrugging her shoulders. 'I know you're frightened, but there's a whole new world for you now, lots of new people to meet. For now, you should try to learn to see the world around you again, and you'll have your family here to keep you safe when you feel scared.'

'Right,' I said, nodding, 'and no evil spirits.'

'No,' she said, tilting her head to one side. 'I wouldn't get too worried on that score. They really are obvious to spot. I'm sure you'll meet some wonderful people, it will be fun.'

Before I could say anything else, she was walking towards the door. 'Take care, Portia,' she said, smiling.

'Thank you, Mary,' I replied, following her to the patio door to see her out. 'I'll see you soon.'

She nodded and was gone. Rather than walking through the door, she had simply faded from the room.

I sat down on the bench where I had been sitting when I had noticed her at the window earlier. I didn't know where to begin.

There should have been a pamphlet. *The Afterlife: The Truth Behind the Veil.* I giggled to myself at the thought. I'd need to suggest it to Mary when I saw her next.

I wasn't smiling for long. The stillness of the house surrounded me. Maybe I would just sit here for a while longer. I had all the time in the world after all.

Chapter Two
Exploration

I didn't know how long I had been sitting in the kitchen, but when I looked out of the patio doors I could see that it was daylight once more and there was snow on the ground. It took me by surprise and I decided to get up and try taking Mary's advice. If I sat in the house any longer, years could pass by and I would still have no idea what I was supposed to be doing.

I walked up the stairs to my room and looked around. It seemed similar to how I remembered it. Nothing appeared to have been touched, but I noticed that there was a thick layer of dust on top of my chest of drawers. I tried to brush my finger along the top. It was as if there was a magnetic force preventing my hand from making contact with the surface. I screwed my eyes up, concentrated and tried again. To my frustration I noticed that I had barely disturbed the surface of the dust. Something to work on, I thought, sighing.

I walked towards my wardrobe to put on a coat before heading outside, purely out of habit, and found that when I thought about putting one on, it simply appeared on my back. It was my favourite navy blue duffle coat with the thick red scarf my mum had given me for Christmas the year before. I had believed it lost, but that didn't seem to be a problem now. Not bad, I thought to myself. Maybe later I'll try a new hair style?

I glanced in the mirror to check my appearance; the first time I had done so since Mary had made me look in a mirror. My almost blonde hair was not enhanced by the now silvery grey hue which shone from it, and my once blue eyes didn't seem to hold the colour they had when I had been alive. To me, they seemed dull and lifeless. I wondered whether ghosts could wear make up. Then I shook my head, what a stupid thought. Surely one of the bonuses to this life would be not worrying about dieting or fashion trends. I touched my hair, it felt normal to me. I touched my face. Again it felt as tangible and soft as it always had. I wasn't cold and to my own touch, I felt completely solid. I don't know what I had been expecting, but I suppose I thought there would be a difference.

As I turned to leave the room I noticed my CD rack and anger swelled up inside me. 'Susan!' I yelled at the top of my voice. I then realised that she wouldn't be able to hear me. Come to think of it, the house felt completely empty again. This didn't quell my anger. The little witch had riffled my CD collection. What a lovely way to honour your newly dead sister! Typical Susan...

I stomped downstairs and walked towards the front door. I remembered that Mary had told me to simply think of a place and I would be there, but I had no idea where I wanted to go, so I thought that perhaps a walk would spark my imagination. I reached out for the door handle and as my hand fought to make contact with the brass, I found myself on the other side of the heavy wooden door. It was a little disconcerting, rather like driving over a hill in the road too quickly. I tried to shrug off the strange feeling in my belly and headed off up the garden path. As with the front door, I found myself on the other side of the gate without actually having to open it.

I wandered along the main road for a while but the crowds in the street made me feel uneasy. I suppose it was just London life, but I had never been particularly comfortable on the crowded pavements. I think it's the kind of city you either adapt to, or you don't. It was like survival of the fittest. Having spent most of my childhood in the town of Whitby on the east coast, I had never taken to the constant buzz of the capital. Even in the height of tourist season, Whitby had never been like this. Even when it was mobbed, an empty corner of the churchyard could always be found.

I kept moving to avoid walking into someone, but the problem was that they didn't do the same for me. While I know that this doesn't differ much from how people walk around the city streets in normal life, it felt like weaving in and around a shoal of tightly bound fish. The difference was that even when they walked right into me, I somehow seemed to come through the other side unscathed. I started closing my eyes when I thought it was going to happen, making the sensation slightly easier. When I did have a collision it felt as if I was being stretched or squashed, I couldn't quite put my finger on it.

Eventually I came to the entrance of the local park and ducked through the gate. The place didn't look particularly busy; I supposed that was because of the weather. It was definitely mid-winter and no-one would want to be out in this cold unless they had to be. That is, except the few determined dog walkers who were dragging their pooches along the path, hoping they would hurry up and complete their daily constitutionals.

It was at this point that I realised I didn't actually feel the cold. I could see the dog walkers shivering and pulling their collars up, breath streaming from their mouths in billowing smoky puffs, but I felt nothing. I didn't feel warm, but I didn't feel cold. It was an extremely odd sensation. I stopped, took a deep breath and let it flow from my mouth; still nothing. I then tried holding my breath. With my first attempt, I felt a great urge to breathe after less than a minute, because it was a natural function of my old body to have air. However, after a few tries at it, I realised I didn't need air at all. Breathing did seem to enhance my senses slightly, I could smell the smoky city streets, but I couldn't feel air filling my lungs. I already knew that I couldn't really touch things properly, or at least, I didn't need to. I wondered whether I could taste. All of the usual fast food vans were shut up tight. There was obviously no point in opening on such a cold and quiet morning. My taste experiment would need to wait until later.

Absentmindedly, watching the birds pecking the hard earth, I walked further along the path towards the canal. I saw a group of sparrows chirruping at one another and hopping along the ground on the path in front of me. They were fighting over some bread which had been scattered by one of the park's visitors. Noticing my approach, they hastily flew away into a nearby tree. At least someone can see me, I thought.

When I arrived at the waterside and sat down on a crystallised frost covered bench, I realised that I had been breathing normally the whole way. Obviously a force of habit, I decided not to worry about that one. It would feel completely alien to walk through the world never breathing. Everything was alien right now; I decided not to add anything else to my list of *strange*.

I sat there for some time, watching the sun rise up in the sky and the people meandering by me. By midday the number of passers-by had increased somewhat; office workers on their lunch hour and children enjoying the afternoon break by throwing snowballs at one another. It was fun in a way. I wanted to see if I could pick up a snow ball and throw it at an unsuspecting child, but then I remembered Mary's words of warning about trying to make contact with the living. I didn't want to break the rules before I had even begun. So instead, I settled down to sit and watch the battle taking place before me. Two local schools, who had obviously arranged to meet for the fight, were frantically trying to arrange their forces to best take down the others. It looked set to be a thrilling encounter.

It was then that I noticed *him*. He was on the other side of the canal and was watching me intently. I don't know why I hadn't seen him before, perhaps he had only arrived, but he stood out like a beacon. He appeared to be someone else like me, someone dead. In the instant I saw him I felt a small flicker of what Mary had been talking about when she said that she had been able to sense me. Seeing another dead person was like sensing a spark of light in the corner of your eye; like sunlight reflecting off a shiny surface for an instant. While I couldn't quite put my finger on why my attention was drawn to it, drawn to him, I felt a mixture of apprehension and joy. Since Mary had left, I had been worrying that I would never find anyone else. Eternity would be a very long time with no-one to talk to. Still, I'd never been the world's best conversationalist. What would I say to him?

The moment he saw me returning his gaze, he dissipated like smoke. In that instant when our eyes met, a look of panic had come over his face, as if he had been caught out doing something covert. I made to shout out as he faded from view, but was too late, he was gone. I realised that while I had been looking at him, everything else in the park seemed to have faded away. I was surrounded by silence, the children and passers by, somehow gone. As he vanished, it was as though someone had turned the volume back up on a television set. I was back where I had been, sitting on a bench, alone in the park. While I had felt a spark of hope at seeing someone else like me, his sudden absence had drained the happiness I had experienced while watching the people pass by and children fighting. Obviously death hadn't improved my social skills.

I rose from the bench and made to walk back towards the exit of the park and the main road. I didn't want to be there anymore. As I walked, I couldn't get the image of this new ghost from my mind. He couldn't have been much older than me, and there was something intense in his stare. His dark brown hair was longer than most boys wore it now and it hung over his face, almost hiding his eyes; sharp blue eyes, the colour still visible even through the grey haze which seemed to cover us. He had been brighter than I was, more alive somehow. Trust me to look mediocre, even in death. There had been something almost beautiful about him, but very sad at the same time. It was an expression which I recognised, even though I didn't know him at all, like he was somehow familiar. Whomever the boy was, he had vanished quickly enough when he had noticed me looking back at him. Come to think of it, I had tended to have that effect on members of the opposite sex when I was alive, why would that change now?

I thrust my hands deep into my pockets an action I would have made when alive, to stave off the cold, and trudged onwards. I couldn't explain why the boy's disappearance had affected me so much. I usually didn't like meeting strangers. Perhaps it was just because I had realised that months had passed without anyone looking at me. That is, until Mary came along. Surely it couldn't mean anything more than that.

I was standing waiting to cross the High Street, completely in a daze, when I noticed another man across the street. He was standing watching me with great interest. Older than the boy I had seen earlier, he must have been at least ten years my senior. He was short, stout, and even with his deathly greyness, I could tell his hair was a thick, greasy auburn tangle. He had messy stubble and sunken dark eyes. His appearance immediately said one thing. Trouble.

The lights changed and I made to cross the street, feeling slightly uncomfortable. The whole time I could feel his unbroken stare following me. I glanced up again as I reached the other side and saw that he was now walking towards me, a toothy grin forming upon his face. I felt the strangest sensation. I realised what I was feeling was that my heart should have been racing, but I didn't have a heart beat. Taken aback by this, I stopped in the street and without meaning to, allowed the man to catch up with me.

'Hello there,' he said, in a thick common accent. 'New?' he asked.

'Erm, yes,' I mumbled. 'How did you know?'

'You don't need to wait for the green man anymore,' he said, smiling at me. Something about his expression told me that he was mocking me.

'Ah,' I said, feeling sheepish, 'lots of new things to remember.' I made to start walking away, but he didn't seem to want to let me go. He held out an arm to bar my way.

'How long have you been with us?' he asked, looking me up and down in a very strange manner. It made me feel uncomfortable, as if I were an animal being examined before purchase.

'I don't know,' I said. As soon as I had spoken I wished I hadn't said this, because his expression seemed to change. It made me feel as if I had to get away from him, quickly. He looked as though he had found a new toy.

'Really?' he said, reaching out to take my arm. 'If you like, I can show you around?'

As he touched me, I felt a strange, cold sensation, the first temperature change I had noticed. I realised this was what fear must feel like. Was this the kind of dark person Mary had been talking about? The atmosphere around us did feel putrid, somehow unnatural.

Before I knew what was happening, I realised that we were standing in a dark, narrow street. 'Where is this?' I asked, sounding breathless.

'This is home,' the man said, grinning. 'Can be home for you too if you like?'

The place was disgusting. Vermin were scuttling around our feet, desperately trying to get away from our presence. Rubbish was piled around us, and I could see some figures moving around in the shadows. 'Who are they?' I asked, my voice now no more than a whisper.

'Them?' he said, looking into the alley. 'Some of them are like us, some of them are alive, but may as well be like us.'

I felt a great urge to run and before I knew it, I was outside my house. To my horror, I found that because he had been touching my arm, he had come along with me.

'Where are we now?' he asked, looking around the street. 'Your home I presume? Very nice indeed, I'd love to come…'

'No…' I interrupted, stuttering, terrified that he would now be able to follow me into the house. 'No, it's not my house. Sorry, I'm new at this. I have to go,' I said, completely petrified, pulling my arm away quickly.

'Not so fast, love,' he said, reaching out to grab me once more. His grin appeared even more menacing that it had earlier.

Before he could get hold of me again, I quickly thought of my home and in an instant I was standing in the middle of my bedroom, panting. Trying to steady my breathing, I looked around the room and found that he had not come with me. I still hadn't gotten used to the change in my body. My silent heart still felt like it should be racing, and the deep breaths I was taking didn't seem to be doing anything to calm the non-existent adrenalin that was rushing through my system.

I chanced a glance out of the bedroom window and saw that he was still standing in the street, looking at the houses intently, obviously trying to work out which one was mine. As he looked up at my house I pulled away from the window quickly, I was sure he had seen me. I closed my eyes to try to keep the fear away; again it felt as if my heart should have been pounding in my chest. When I opened them again it was night time outside and my room was in complete darkness. I decided to have one more look in the hope that the shadows would hide me. The street was now completely empty save for the parked cars and the orange glow of the street lamps; relief flooded through me.

I then heard voices downstairs and decided to see who was home. While my house hadn't felt as though it had held a proper family for some time, I had a great desire to see the people I had once been so close to. My afternoon had given me a desperate yearning for something familiar. I walked towards the door and before I knew it, was standing in the dimly-lit living room.

My sister Susan was sitting in the armchair in the corner, her arms folded and her mouth set in a severe line. Dad was sitting in his usual chair by the fire with a glass of whisky in his hand. He looked somehow older than I remembered him. Obviously I hadn't been paying attention to what had been happening around here lately. He stared into the flames with hard eyes. It was easy to taste the hostile atmosphere in the air. There was something almost metallic about it. I would need to get used to my new senses. Emotions seemed to be tangible somehow.

'I don't care, Susan,' he said bitterly. 'You're not going. Can you please stop going on about this? I'm not going to change my mind.'

'But, Dad,' she whined, 'it's not fair. You used to let Portia go.'

'Don't,' Dad said, wincing. The sound of my name looked to have caused him physical pain. 'Just, don't, okay?'

'It's just a concert, Dad. It's in the local theatre, everyone goes when it's on.'

'Well,' he sighed, 'you're not everyone are you?'

'If you had your way, I'd be no-one,' she muttered sulkily. 'Just ask Portia.'

'What is that supposed to mean?' he asked, angrily glowering at his daughter.

'Nothing,' she mumbled. She then got up and stormed out of the room, slamming the living room door behind her.

Dad followed her with his eyes, and then turned his gaze back towards the fire. A tear rolled down his cheek and he threw his glass into the hearth. It shattered and the flames flared as the alcohol sprayed everywhere. He rose from his chair and stalked into the kitchen.

I stood there for a long time, feeling completely lost. The dad I had grown used to in recent months didn't seem to care about anything. Susan seemed to have been coming and going as she pleased. How much time had passed? I definitely needed to learn how to focus myself. Things had deteriorated, Dad looked like a zombie.

I walked into the kitchen and saw him standing against the counter, staring at the floor. He stood there for a very long time, his eyes empty of all emotion, he looked more dead than I did.

Susan eventually walked into the room and clicked on the kettle. 'I'm sorry, dad,' she said, touching his arm. 'I didn't mean it.'

He pulled his arm away at her touch and gave her a sharp glance. It was as though her hand had burned him. I wanted him to hug her, to hug me. Instead he stared at her coldly for several moments, as if he wasn't sure who she was. 'Do what you like,' he eventually said, blankly. 'You usually do. Besides, this family ended the day your mother walked out the door. I think Portia probably had the right idea.'

Susan seemed to crumple at his words. I couldn't understand why he was being so hateful. They needed one another, I needed them. He walked out of the room and left Susan sobbing to herself.

I felt completely alone. There was no comfort in this house at all. Somehow this made something snap inside me, like a key turning in a lock. I had opened myself to a new kind of fear. The fear of having no shelter, having nowhere to feel loved. A sense of panic washed over me. This was supposed to be my safe haven, the place I would be able to come to when I felt scared. There didn't seem to be any love left. I had no-where and no-one. How was I supposed to make this existence work? I was going to spend eternity in this hopeless pit of despair.

Then I felt it, a cold sensation running down the back of my neck. Again, it completely stunned me. When you didn't feel temperature at all, this sense of panic and fear was like having a bucket of iced water poured over you. Somehow, I knew what I was going to see before I even turned round. Someone was here, someone like me. I spun round to look out of the patio doors, hoping against hope that Mary was the presence I could feel, even though I knew it couldn't be. This wasn't the sparkle in my peripheral vision I had felt when I had seen that young ghost, this was pure dread. Instead of my new friend, standing with his face pressed against the glass was the man I had run away from earlier that day. He was staring at me intently with a leering grin upon his face. It made him look like a beast, his mouth slavering and his eyes hungry.

'Why don't you let me in?' he asked, his fingers scraping against the glass. The noise was incredibly high-pitched. I saw that where his hand touched the window, a cold icy frost seemed to have formed. A ghoulish frozen silhouette of his fingers remained and everything about him oozed evil. The hand print left on the door was a visible manifestation of his cold dead heart.

I backed away from the kitchen, hoping that the heat of the living room would banish him, that he was only drawn here because of my upset and fear. Maybe if I could calm myself, he would go away. It was then that I saw Susan. She was staring at the patio doors with a look of complete horror upon her face. What could she see? Could she see the hand print? Surely she couldn't see the horrid spectre standing just beyond the glass? In that instant I hoped, I didn't want my little sister to see this. She may have annoyed the hell out of me, but she didn't deserve to see this creature.

'Portia?' she asked, whispering it so as not to let dad hear. 'Is that you? What are you doing? I thought I felt you before, are you trying to frighten me? I know I touched your stuff, but it was only because I was missing you.'

I stared between Susan and the figure in the garden, I was petrified. I didn't know how to get rid of him and I couldn't believe that my sister thought this thing was me. I would never try to scare them. The only good thing was that I knew she couldn't actually see him, I wouldn't wish this sight upon anyone.

'I think your sister wants me to come in,' the man said mockingly, slapping his other hand against the glass. 'Why don't you be a good girl and say the words. It's easy, just invite me in. I have some fun games we could play. You're new at this, you need someone like me.'

As his hand had slapped the glass, Susan had become even more petrified, as though the noise and confirmed her fears. She ran from the kitchen and straight past my dad to get away from the foul creature; the creature she believed to be me.

'What's going on?' dad asked, startled by her running past and by the expression on Susan's face. Completely drained of all colour, she almost looked as grey as I did.

The man was now banging on the glass intermittently, obviously loving the terror he was instilling in me and my family. Dad heard the noise and walked into the kitchen to see what had startled Susan. He quickly realised the noise was coming from the garden and flicked the outside light on, intently staring out into the darkness. The man was standing on the other side of the glass making rude gestures towards my unseeing dad.

Hissing and spitting at him like a crazed dog, he looked utterly demonic. I could sense the hairs on the back of my dad's neck stand up and he began to back away from the door, unsure what was making him feel so uneasy.

'Time to play,' the ghost said, his face changing into something even more ghastly, his features becoming more animal-like.

It was clear that he wanted into the house to terrorise me and to scare my family. I couldn't let that happen, but I had no idea what to do. I had led this creature to the place I was supposed to hide in. Staring at my dad, and hearing my sister weeping upstairs, I was frozen with fear. I had to do something, but what?

Finally I had an idea. 'Mary!' I yelled at the top of my voice. 'Help me! Please!'

Chapter Three
Flee From Fright

Time seemed to stand still. I was starting to think no-one was coming to help me. The only thing which marked its passing was the periodic banging on the window pane from the ghost outside. It was like the ticking of some horrific clock, each noise marking out another second when I was alone and unable to help my family. The terror was extraordinary. I don't think I had ever felt anything like it in my living life. Even when my mum left, it was despair I experienced, not this. Nothing like this.

I couldn't tear my eyes from my dad. He stood completely frozen; his mind desperately trying to fathom what could be causing the hideous noises, trying to find a rational explanation. I realised for the first time since this whole experience had started, that I wasn't breathing. I wanted to be as silent as I possibly could. It reminded me of hiding as a child. Somehow I felt that if I was quiet enough, this strange creature would leave us all alone. It was me he wanted, after all.

I knew it wouldn't work, I could almost feel the fear emanating from me like a beacon. The only comfort I could draw from this, was that like my sister, my dad couldn't see him. With every moment that passed, I could sense this creature becoming stronger, feeding off me. The sensation made me feel weak. I noticed that the space around me appeared dimmer; it was as if the fear was lessening my grip on the earth somehow, making my existence a little less tangible.

The noises suddenly stopped and the room was filled with a deathly silence, dad wasn't breathing either. It was as though time had completely ground to a halt; both of us stood there, unmoving. I looked back towards the window and saw that the ghost had vanished. Hoping that this meant the creature had moved on, I looked around the room. While I knew he couldn't have gotten in, I didn't quite trust my new found sense of judgement; this felt too easy. He wouldn't just give up, surely? My fear subsided as I scanned the place; it was just dad and me in the room. He appeared to have calmed down too, still staring out into the darkness. Even his dull human senses seemed to know the creature was no longer at the window. The atmosphere in the kitchen was different. Whatever spell the creature had cast upon us had been momentarily broken.

It was then I heard a banging sound from upstairs. In an instant, I was standing in Susan's room and saw her huddled on her bed, holding a pillow over her face to block out the noise. She was rocking back and forth and weeping into her bedding. The ghoul was now outside her window, scraping and banging against the glass, his face full of glee at the sight of Susan's distress. He seemed to be growing brighter with each passing minute. His red eyes glowing, I could swear they were growing larger. Like headlights, I could feel them blinding me.

He pressed his face against window pane when he saw me appear. 'Open up, little girl,' he spat, looking straight at me. 'Come on, we can have fun if you let me in. I didn't like that you tried to hide from me earlier, I was only trying to be friendly. Don't you want to be friends? No-one else is going to befriend you, you need me. Come on, just let me in!' BANG, BANG, BANG! The glass shook in its frame.

Susan shuddered at the sound.

I needed to do something, anything. Mary wasn't here. A little voice in my head told me she wasn't coming. 'No,' I said, trying to muster my courage. 'You're not welcome here. Leave us alone!' I knew I didn't sound remotely convincing. When the words came out, they sounded nothing more than a whisper. His presence was sapping every ounce of strength from my being.

'Portia, please stop this...' Susan muttered, her words muffled by the pillow over her head. 'Please don't do this to us. Please...'

I looked at her aghast. She thought I was the one doing this to them.

'It looks like I'm getting you into trouble,' the ghost said, gleefully pressing his face up against the glass once more. 'Girly thinks her dead sister is rapping on the window pane? A bit of a cliché, but if it gets me through the door, I don't care.' He grimaced. 'Let me in, let me in...' he chanted, putting on a mock female voice. It sounded completely warped coming from such a creature's mouth. 'Come on, girly, let me in... I can be your new best friend, come on, girly, let me in...'

I looked away from him, I didn't want to see his vile, putrid face. In the darkness his pupils seemed to glow bright red, like an animal's eyes reflecting light in the dark. I turned to my sister. 'It's not me, Susan,' I said to her, feeling utter frustration that she couldn't hear my words, couldn't sense me in the room. It somehow made me feel claustrophobic, as though I were trapped, unable to reach her. If she couldn't feel me through the veil, how could she feel this creature?

'Come on,' he said, his voice suddenly full of encouragement. 'That's it.'

I looked back at the window. To my horror, the ghost wasn't looking at me anymore. He was looking directly at Susan. She took the pillow from her face and rose from the bed. Walking towards the window, her face told me that every step she took was terrifying her. It reminded me how young she still was. In the dimly lit room, she looked like a little girl, my little sister.

'No, Susan, stop!' I yelled, willing her to hear me. She continued her trance like procession towards the window and the creature that was slathering at the thought of gaining entry to the room. 'Don't!' I turned to the window, 'What are you doing to her? Whatever you're doing, stop it right now!'

'She's just being friendly, unlike you,' he said, a thick raspy laugh escaping his lips. 'She wants to let her poor dead sister back into the house. I won't disappoint her. This kind of thing is my specialty. I can read what they want like I'm reading a book. Just you wait to see what I have planned for you, you little witch! I'm going to play you like a puppet. Teach you to show some respect for your elders.'

Susan's hand reached for the handle on the window. 'Portia...' she muttered. 'If I let you in, you have to stop this. Please...'

'I'll behave, girly,' the ghost said, scraping his nails down the glass. The noise made Susan shudder, but she still reached out for the handle, her hand shaking violently.

'No!' I screamed, instinctively reaching forward to touch her hand and stop her before she could open the window. Although it passed straight through, the contact seemed to make her pull her hand away as though it had burned her. Had she felt me?

'Stop interfering,' the man spat. 'I'll find a way whether you like it or not. Your little sister is an easy target. She'll let me in.'

Suddenly I felt another presence. Mary was standing beside me. It was strange, but the creature had been warping my view of everything. I had started to doubt Mary. Had she tricked me before just to get into the house? Did she care about me at all?

As soon as she was here with me in the room, I knew none of this was true. Her being emanated goodness.

'Thank God,' I said, reaching out and taking her hand. 'I called for you so long ago. I didn't think you were coming.'

'Well, that's a nice welcome,' she said, looking around the room. 'I came as quickly as I could. What's going on?' she asked. Her face filled with horror as she noticed the spectre outside the window.

'He followed me here,' I said. 'He wants to get in. I think he's controlling Susan somehow. She seems to think he's me. What do we do? I managed to stop her from opening the window, but she can't hear me.'

'This is bad,' Mary muttered. 'We need to stop her before she opens that window. If he gets in, it'll be nigh on impossible to get him back out.'

'But how can we?' I asked desperately. 'You told me I couldn't try to make contact with the living. I accidentally touched her hand, you should have seen her face. I don't want to do that again. Besides, what about the rules you mentioned before?'

'Rules were made to be broken,' Mary said, hurriedly looking at Susan. 'Stand close and speak to her. You need to convince her that this thing isn't you. You're the only one who'll be able to reach her. She should recognise your presence; you're her flesh and blood. If you can get through to her, she'll know this *thing* isn't you.'

Susan had recovered from my first attempt to stop her and was now reaching out once more for the handle of the window. I walked forward carefully and touched her shoulder. She gasped. 'Susan, it's me,' I whispered. 'Don't open the window. That isn't me. I'm right here, I'm with you. Don't be scared, he can't get in if you don't open the window.'

Susan closed her eyes and tears ran down her face. 'If you're with me now, Portia, you need to stop this. You're scaring us. Things are hard enough. You got away from all this, but I'm still stuck here. I can't deal with this as well, it's not fair.'

'I'm sorry,' I said. 'I didn't mean to leave... I don't know how I left...' I could feel a tear on my own cheek. It was a strange sensation, somehow different to crying when alive. The emotion was there, the feeling in my throat, but the tear itself just felt like a tiny blast of ice-cold air gently caressing my cheek. Again, as it had when my heart was racing, I felt a strange new manifestation of an emotion, but without the physical response which should go with it.

My dad was now standing in the doorway. 'Susan, what are you doing?' he asked, his face ashen white. 'Who were you talking to? If that was you downstairs, this isn't funny. Stop all this at once. You can't start messing around like this, just because you aren't getting your own way. Tell your little friends to back off at once, or I'll call the police.'

She turned and stared at him, looking right through me. It was as though she didn't understand what he was saying. 'I don't know what this is, Dad. It definitely isn't me. How could you think this was me?' Her voice trailed off as the true meaning of my father's words sunk in. 'This isn't normal, Dad,' she continued, finding her voice once more. 'I heard you downstairs, you can feel it too. Someone's here and it isn't any one of my little *friends*.'

'I don't know what's happening,' he said, raising his hand to his forehead. 'It's probably just the wind or cats fighting. The weather has been pretty rough lately.'

'It's not bloody wind, Dad!' she said, frustrated. 'It's her, she's here. I know it. It's Portia! She was trying to get in at the window, and then she was here. She was standing right here! I felt her!' Susan was waving her hand around in the space in which I was standing. I instinctively backed away. While I couldn't feel her hand, its movement inside of me made me feel dizzy, like having little butterflies in my tummy. I noticed her gasp; she could still feel me.

'See,' she said, looking at him angrily. 'Come here, stand here and feel this. It's absolutely freezing in this spot.'

I backed further across the room.

'Damn,' she muttered, 'it's gone. This isn't normal, Dad.'

'Shh…' My dad said, rushing forward and pulling her into his arms. 'Don't say such things. Don't…' he whispered, stroking her hair. 'It's fine. We'll be fine. Portia is gone, I know you miss her, but this isn't going to bring her back.'

'Dad… I…' Susan stuttered, struggling to speak through her tears. 'I'm not lying, Dad,' she sobbed. 'I really think that…'

'I know, honey, I know.' He was trying his best to comfort her, something he should have done a long time ago.

The being outside the window was still there. His face was livid, but he seemed to have lost some of his strength. Obviously the reduction in our fear levels and the heartfelt emotions between Susan and my dad had diminished his power over us.

'I think it's time you left,' Mary said sternly, looking directly at the ghoul. 'You know you are not welcome here. There is nothing for you in this place.'

'Who's gonna make me?' the beast asked leeringly, looking from Mary to myself. 'A newcomer who doesn't know what she wants and some little fairy princess who thinks she's in charge? I'm really scared!' He pulled a face and slapped the window angrily.

I anxiously looked towards my family, but they hadn't noticed the noise this time. I didn't know whether this was just part of the spirit losing its hold over us, or whether they were simply too wrapped up in one another to hear anything going on around them.

'We're not alone,' Mary said confidently. She was clearly disgusted by the creature's display. 'I'm sure we could show you the error of your ways; time for a change of heart perhaps? We belong here, but I'm pretty sure your name would have been on a different list. You wouldn't want me to call upon my friends, would you?'

He danced around the window, obviously trying to scare Mary off. She stood unwavering, staring back at him. When he realised she wasn't leaving, he stopped and stared back. 'Bloody do-gooders,' he said, spitting on the window. The spit turned instantly to ice when it hit the glass. 'If you get bored sitting around doing nothing, girly, you know where to find me.' He blew a kiss at me and I felt myself shiver as he did it.

With that, he was gone. The atmosphere in the room immediately changed, it lifted somehow. The fear was gone. It made me feel better in myself.

My dad and Susan were still locked in an embrace, both crying. It seemed to be the first time either of them had let their guard down. I felt lonely, as if I were being left out somehow. I knew this wasn't fair, especially since I must have caused this situation, or at least part of it. My death obviously hadn't made my mum feel guilty enough to come back and these two were in a complete mess.

'Right, young lady,' Mary said, turning to me, looking like an angry school mistress. It shook me from my train of thought. 'What exactly have you been doing to end up in this mess? I leave you alone for a second and you lure a ghoul back to your house? They aren't exactly the best kind of company to keep. I thought I warned you against…'

'I didn't do anything,' I cut in defensively. 'I went out *exploring* like you told me to. That *man* saw me in the street and then followed me here. What did he want?'

'Exactly what you were thinking,' Mary said, sighing. 'He wanted you to let him in. He could have had free reign of the house if invited, terrifying your family and destroying you. It's what creatures like him feed off, fear.'

'Destroying me...' I muttered.

'Not literally,' she said shaking her head. 'Once you're here in this form you're more or less indestructible. He would have broken your spirit though, made you his slave. They prey upon the weak and the new among us. That's one of the reasons I came to help you in the first place. If we are to exist here safely we have to limit the numbers beasts like him are able to recruit, although I use the word *recruit* in its loosest sense. They're more like vultures. They eat away at you, until you're nothing but a shadow of who you should have been. A flicker, rather than the burning light you could be.'

She saw the expression on my face.

'Don't panic,' she said, touching my face. 'I'm sure you'll be fine. You haven't exactly had the nicest introduction to this life have you?'

'I'm sorry,' I said, sinking down on Susan's bed. I heard a gasp and noticed that Susan had looked around. As I had sat down, the mattress had moved. I held my breath.

'Come,' Mary said, taking my arm. 'I think you've caused enough trouble for one night. Let's talk elsewhere, before you drive your poor sister completely insane.'

We were now standing in the kitchen and I was still feeling shaken by everything that had happened. 'I must have looked so obvious out on the street,' I muttered, still trying to explain things to Mary. 'He said he noticed me because I waited for the traffic lights before crossing the road. I didn't know, I didn't think...'

Mary laughed, 'A beginner's mistake. Although not one I have to worry about. We all behave in ways which feel normal to us. It takes time before you learn to blend in. We didn't have such contraptions in my time, so I don't feel bound to live by them.'

'I'm surprised I'm not a natural,' I said. 'I spent my whole life blending in. I wasn't exactly the type to stand out in a crowd. I'm just finding this all so difficult. When I'm in this house, time seems to slip away from me. I don't know how long I've been dead, but I know I finished school. That means at least six months have passed without me so much as noticing. I don't want to carry on this way. I don't think I can do this all by myself.'

'Time tends to do that,' she said, trying to comfort me. 'Look at it this way. It's as if you're in a daze, day dreaming. When you're like this, time can pass as quickly as it likes. If something catches your attention, a bird on a branch or a person you love entering a room it pulls you out of your daze and focuses you in a specific time. The only moments we move at the same pace as humans, are when we are interested in them and their world. Other than that, we move on our own plane.'

I stared at her blankly, having never felt so completely out of my depth. I felt like a child. 'Can I come with you?' I asked, hoping this time Mary wouldn't leave me behind once more. I didn't want to be alone again. 'Eternity is going to be a long time on my own. Look who I managed to bump into on my first venture out of doors. The only way for me not to screw this up, is to hide in here completely alone and the thought of that is unbearable. You saw how things are, my family isn't exactly the best comfort at the moment, and I don't think I'm helping them either.'

She sighed. 'I still don't think it's the best time for you to be leaving your family. You can't cause all this and then walk out on them. They could to go crazy, or leave here completely. You never know when you might need them.'

'I don't think dad would leave. I think he still hopes my mum will come back. Besides, I think I might be causing more problems by staying,' I mumbled, sitting down at the kitchen table. 'I'm useless.'

'Perhaps you're right,' she said, touching her forehead.

I glanced up, hurt.

'Not about the useless part,' she added reassuringly. 'All I mean is, you can't stay trapped in here, and I don't want you wandering the streets alone getting yourself into trouble. I will let you come with me. Only if you promise that you will stop by and check on your family regularly. You need this kind of contact to ground you. If you rush into things, you will end up feeling alien in this world. I won't have you losing your humanity. That man who was here tonight is probably a soul who didn't have memories of love to guide him. Never mind the fact that he may decide to pay them a return visit. You owe them our protection. Besides, eternity is a long time to spend without your family. I can vouch for that. They may only be so accessible to you for a short time, don't squander it.'

'Okay,' I said, looking up at her. 'I'll visit them, just please don't leave me alone again. This whole thing happened because I tried to go out on my own.'

'We all start out that like that,' Mary said, frowning. 'You need to find your own way, but I empathise. I was left alone at too young an age. Still, I cannot protect you from everything.'

'I know,' I said, smiling sadly. 'I don't think you're completely safe anywhere, any of us, I mean.'

'That's a sad way to look at life, or should I say, death,' Mary said, touching my shoulder. 'Let's go. Perhaps if I introduce you to some nicer people, you won't be quite so petrified of the world around you.'

I looked up at her, scared once more. I didn't want Mary to leave me, but I was also scared at the prospect of meeting her friends.

'Not everyone is out to get you,' she added, misunderstanding my fear. 'The majority of our kind exist in peace.'

'Our kind,' I muttered.

'I know it's not nice to think of,' she said, squeezing my shoulder, 'but you are not one of them anymore. If you're lucky, they will join you in this life, one day. Until then, you learn to live your own way. You visit them to feel their love.'

'Thanks,' I said, putting my hand into hers. I felt a strange sense of peace as soon as we were touching one another. 'I promise I will, but I really need your help...' I was cut off in a gasp. We had moved and this time it felt different. The feeling in my tummy multiplied, after several seconds we were still in darkness. I didn't know whether we were still travelling or whether I was surrounded by complete blackness. This time, moving made me want to scream.

Chapter Four
When A House Is A Home

I knew we were no longer in my kitchen, but I wasn't sure where we were exactly. It was the first time a shift had taken any length of time. It had probably only been a matter of seconds, but in my panic, it seemed to last an eternity. As I felt my feet hit the earth, I thought I was going to be sick. Could you get travel sickness in the afterlife? Yet again, it seemed to be a reaction that my human side held on to, even though my body no longer felt the sensation. I doubted it would be possible for someone like me to be sick; at least I hoped so.

My legs almost gave way beneath me, but Mary supported my weight. I liked her touch. As I glanced up in the darkness looking for her eyes, I realised why. When one dead person touched another, you felt it. Not heat, but you felt the touch. It felt soft and it felt solid. I hadn't had that kind of contact until Mary had come along. I hadn't realised what it meant until I had met my ghoul friend; it was a great comfort. I also realised that, even in the dark, I could see Mary perfectly, every detail. She stood out, even in the blackness that surrounded us. Having never really been in such darkness with another ghost, I'd never seen a spirit as a beacon. I wondered what it would have felt like if I had seen the boy in the park at night. If he looked anything like Mary, he wouldn't be a spark in my peripheral vision. She seemed to light everything around us. I wondered whether she had been glowing this brightly before; perhaps I was just learning to see.

Slowly, my eyes adjusted and I noticed that we were outside. I could smell moisture and wood and could hear birds and creatures nearby. Mary, who still held my hand, gave me a tug to get me to start walking. I could sense gravel crunching beneath my feet and see the moon above us. We stopped walking and I saw that we were standing in front of an old abandoned house. It was hard to make out any detail since the whole place was in complete darkness. It looked like a shadowy ruin which had long since been empty.

'Is this where you live?' I asked. The place smelled old and unloved.

'Yes,' she said proudly. 'Welcome to Havenshaw Manor.' She then looked round and saw the expression on my face and looked rather offended. 'It's all about perspective. This used to be a very grand house. I remember it from my living years. Now, it's a little uncared for, but it gives us a place where we can dwell in greater number. This in turn makes it somewhere we can protect.'

'I see,' I said, trying my best to look impressed. 'I'm sure it's lovely inside.'

She shook her head. 'Come along.'

'Wait,' I whispered, hesitating. 'If it's as dark in there as it is out here, I won't be able to see a thing.' I knew that the statement sounded strange, considering my senses told me that I should be able to see in the dark.

'Yes you will,' Mary replied, sighing. 'You keep holding onto these human behaviours. You think you can't see in the dark, so you can't. Open your eyes!'

I closed my eyes and tried to think about what she said; I should be able to see. When I opened them again I almost gasped aloud. I could see everything. It wasn't like standing in daylight, but I could still make out everything around me: the gravel path, the overgrown lawn and the thick forest of trees off in the distance. The world had a lot less colour, but I could still see it as clearly as if the sun were shining. I felt a bit like a cat, skulking in the dark. 'So we don't need daylight to see,' I muttered.

'Well,' Mary mused, it does help, but it's not essential. 'You will always be able to see better during the day, but it's not important. It just adds a different tone to things, a splash of colour. You can get by quite as easily at night. If you couldn't, this life would be rather difficult, don't you think?'

'Isn't it difficult anyway?' I asked.

She sighed once more. 'We don't sleep, Portia. If we couldn't see, we would spend half our time bumbling around in the dark.'

'Right,' I said, nodding. What she was saying made sense, in a strange way. 'Although it would explain things that go *bump* in the night,' I said, making a feeble attempt at a joke to hide my nervousness.

'Very amusing,' she said, sounding once more like a school mistress. 'Anyway,' she continued, starting forward once more, 'enough of this. Come into the house and let me do the talking. I'll need to introduce you to the others. They're not used to newcomers. We haven't had someone new join us for years now.'

'How long have you been... this way?' I asked hesitantly, struggling to find the right words to describe our situation.

'I'm not exactly sure,' she replied. 'As you will have noticed, when you're new at this, time moves all on its own. I know that I wasn't born in this century, probably early in the last or perhaps late in the one before that. I remember Queen Victoria being on the throne, although I was rather young when she passed on. Before you ask,' she added looking at me sideways, 'I haven't met her here. I'm assuming that she was important enough to warrant a free ticket.'

'Wow,' I said, considering the thought of existing for so long and ignoring her jibe about long dead royalty. 'This world must seem so strange to you.'

'Not really,' Mary mused. 'When you have lived this way for as long as I have, you stop noticing changes in the human world. They don't matter; it's the people who count. No matter how long this world lasts, fundamentally, people don't change.'

I nodded blankly, not having either the experience or perspective yet to agree or disagree with her. My human life had shown me that people could be pretty crappy. If that was what she meant then this existence wasn't going to be much better than my last one.

As she went to walk through the doorway I hesitated.

'Don't worry, Portia,' she said, smiling. 'I know it will be strange for you to meet so many of us, but I hope that it will be a pleasant experience. You need to learn not to be so scared all the time. If anything, that kind of behaviour attracts the wrong kind of people. We will try to build your confidence before you head back out into the world.'

I smiled nervously, once more experiencing the extremely disconcerting sensation of my heart racing without actually beating. I didn't know whether I would ever get used to that.

Suddenly we were through the doorway. It was a large, once impressive entranceway. There were several heavy wooden doors leading off to the left and right and a grand staircase in the centre. It looked as if the banister was broken in places and some of the steps were missing, but this was unlikely to cause problems for people who could flit from room to room. The place was actually very fitting. It was a bit like us, slightly grey and dusty. I could imagine how beautiful a house it would have been when it was alive.

I glanced around, preparing myself for hordes of people, but no-one was there. It was a bit of an anti-climax. When Mary had said it would be hard to meet so many new people, I had expected the place to be packed to the rafters. 'Where is everyone?' I whispered.

'I don't know,' she whispered back, giggling at my nervousness. 'They're probably upstairs. Let's go into the lounge and I'll call them.'

We walked into a large room at the end of the hall. There looked to be some grand pieces of furniture which had been covered with white sheets, although several sofas were uncovered. As we entered the room, a figure appeared by the fire place. He was tall and broad in stature, with curly dark hair and chiselled features. In age, he looked to be no older than his mid thirties. Wearing a shirt with an embellished frilly collar, his face spread into a wide grin when he saw Mary.

'You're home, love,' he said. 'I sensed you come in.'

He looked to me as though he was physically relieved she was back. As he gazed upon her, his brown eyes sparkled.

'Henry,' Mary said, a smile spreading across her perfect lips. 'Portia,' she said addressing me in a strangely formal way, 'this is my husband, Henry.'

'Henry Leveson-Bass, the third,' he said, crossing the room in a couple of large strides. 'It is a pleasure to meet you, Miss Portia.' He took my hand and kissed it. If I had been alive, I would have blushed.

'Trouble?' he asked, looking at his wife with concern.

'Nothing I couldn't handle,' she said dismissively.

He touched her face gently.

She seemed to glow for a moment, his touch giving her pleasure. 'I didn't want to leave her alone. I think she's going to need our help to find her way.'

'Of course,' Henry said, smiling at me once more. 'Welcome to Havenshaw, you are most welcome here.'

I nodded gratefully. I didn't know what to say to the man. I had never met anyone like him. It was like trying to have a conversation with Mr Darcy. Dashing, was probably the most accurate word, although even then it didn't quite do him justice.

'Are the others around?' Mary asked.

'Mostly,' Henry replied. 'I'm sure a new arrival in the house won't have escaped their notice.'

Mary looked up to the ceiling and simply cleared her throat. She then turned to me and gave me a reassuring smile.

One by one, spirits began to appear in the room. There were four others in total. They seemed to vary in age. There was an older man who looked to be in his sixties. He reminded me of someone from a Dickens novel. He had rather large sideburns, longish hair and a suit with a tailed jacket. He was eying me suspiciously from across the room, but had the type of face where it was difficult to tell if he was scowling or not. He made me think of the breed of dog which has folds of skin and jowls. I tried to smile back, but he didn't respond.

Then there was a woman who appeared to be middle aged. Slightly rotund, she had a very cheerful demeanour. In life I could imagine her having strawberry blonde hair and rosy cheeks. She wore a twin set and pearls, with a knee length tweed skirt. She had obviously lived in the nineteen fifties or around that time.

The other two ghosts stood very close together. They were a boy and a girl and they appeared to be of a similar age to myself. The girl was petite and seemed shy. She had very dark hair and large blue eyes. Her hair was braided and pinned so that it framed her face; I couldn't quite place what era she was from, she wore a long dark dress, but it was very plain. The boy had his face hidden and all I could see was that his hair was dark.

'Everyone,' Mary said, smiling, 'this is, Portia. She's new to this life and I told her we would help her to settle in.'

The older gentleman cleared his throat. 'Do we have room for another stray, Mary? Will you continually bring your little *projects* back to our home?'

'Of course we have room,' the rotund woman said, tutting under her breath. She turned and beamed at me. 'Welcome to the manor, my dear. It's a pleasure to meet you. I'm sure you'll be very happy here.'

I nodded to her, smiling gratefully. When the old man had spoken I felt a lump rise in my throat. What would I do if they didn't want me here?

'I'm Betsy,' she continued, and this is, Mr Weatherby.'

The old man made to doff his non existent cap but didn't speak.

'Don't mind him,' Betsy said, 'he's a bit of an acquired taste, but we like him.'

I couldn't help smiling at her. She was a kind person, it exuded from every inch of her being.

'I'm Beth,' the dark haired girl said meekly. She smiled at me with a sense of hope and something about her expression reminded me of myself. I think she wanted a friend. 'This is my brother, David,' she continued, giving the boy beside her a nudge.

He didn't raise his head.

'Don't be rude, David,' Betsy said. I got the impression that she was the "mother" of the group, someone who had been used to dealing with children during her earthly existence.

The boy finally looked up and glanced at me. Shocked, I heard myself gasp. It was the boy who had been watching me in the park, the one who had vanished before my eyes, he didn't smile. He looked very serious, but curious at the same time. For a second I could have sworn that he recognised me too, but his eyes changed and looked very controlled. He looked as though he was trying to appear disinterested.

'Hello,' he said eventually. The delay between Betsy telling him off and his actually speaking to me was awkward.

'Hello,' I mumbled.

Mary, who had moved over and was standing with Henry behind her, his arms wrapped around her waist, was curious about my reaction to the boy. 'Have you two met before?' she asked, something devilish in her expression. I felt as if she knew something I didn't.

'No,' he cut in defensively, before I could answer, 'of course not.'

'Right,' Mary said, winking at me. 'Well, anyway, I hope you'll all make Portia welcome. She's had a bit of a rough start and needs some help. Beth, perhaps you would show her to an empty room that she can have for herself?'

'Yes,' the girl replied. If she hadn't been so grey, I would have sworn she was blushing. She gently crossed the floor and took my hand. 'Would you like a tour?'

'That would be nice,' I said, holding her small hand tightly. It was strange, but when she touched me, I felt a slight sense of warmth; something I hadn't had with Mary. I dismissed this thought, presuming that I must not have noticed it with Mary; perhaps it was because we had been outside. This girl's hand made me feel exactly like it would have felt to take someone's hand when I was alive. It was a lovely sensation.

Without walking, we were back out in the hall and I could hear that the discussion was still going on in the room behind us. It made me feel uncomfortable. Were they complaining about my arrival? The old man hadn't seemed particularly happy to see me.

'I don't know,' I heard him say, 'another child?'

'She's hardly a child,' Betsy scolded. 'She's a young lady, and besides, did you see the look of her? She's barely a whisper of smoke; she needs help if she's going to build her strength. I don't know that I've ever seen a soul looking quite so pale, there was barely a glow about her, poor little urchin.'

Beth cleared her throat at this. She could obviously feel my hurt at Betsy's words and was trying to distract me. 'This way,' she said, holding her free arm out to direct me down the corridor.

We started to walk along the dark passage and I could see that there were at least four more doors on this section of the ground floor. The young girl was humming to herself as she walked, I assumed to make sure that we couldn't make out any more of the conversation from the lounge. Beth walked to the closest door on our right.

'I think you'll like living here,' she said, passing through the door. After a moment's hesitation I followed behind. 'This is my favourite place, it's the music room.'

I could see a large piano in the corner, and some other furniture which still had sheets over the top. 'Can you play the piano?' I asked.

'Yes,' she said, meekly, 'although we can't really keep it properly tuned so it doesn't always sound so good.'

'Can I hear?' I asked.

'I...' she stuttered. 'I don't usually play when someone else is in the room.'

'You don't have to if you don't want to,' I said, smiling reassuringly.

'Thank you,' she replied, smiling back.

I walked over to the piano and pressed down on one of the keys, disappointed that the young girl didn't want to play for me. It took some effort, but I was able to make it move. The sound was incredibly soft, but I guessed that was because of me.

'You'll get stronger,' she said, seeing the strain on my face.

I looked up inquisitively.

'When you get more used to this life,' she continued, 'you get better at these things. It gets easier to touch stuff.'

I smiled.

'What would you like to see next?' she asked. 'There's also a library and the kitchens on this floor. There's a dining room, but no-one goes in there very often. I don't think they like to be reminded of something they can't have.

'I'd like to see the library,' I replied, smiling. I liked this girl, I didn't know why.

'Great,' she said, smiling back at me. 'I like that room too.'

She took my hand and we were standing in the middle of a large, darkened room lined with books. I walked along the shelves, touching the spines. 'Why are all these books still here? Wouldn't the house have been emptied?'

'No,' she said, walking quietly along behind me. 'Mr Weatherby owned the house when he was alive. When his wife died, he became a bit of a hermit. They say that he died of a broken heart,' her voice now no more than a whisper. 'His final wish was that the house would be completely closed up and nothing touched.'

'That's sad,' I mused.

'Yes,' she replied. 'But it's good for us. We have somewhere which still has some comforts, but at the same time, no-one ever comes here. Some of the locals are convinced it's haunted.' She waggled her fingers at me in a mock spooky motion.

I smiled. I suppose this was one instance where the local stories were definitely true. 'I'm surprised he let you all in if he wanted to be left alone, wouldn't he want to be alone in death?'

'I think he did, at first,' she said. 'He hoped his wife would be here, that they could live in the house together forever.'

'But she's not...' I muttered.

'No,' Beth said, looking sad. 'She's not. I like to think she got to cross over. There are paintings of her in the house. She was a very beautiful woman, she had kind eyes. According to David, the locals think that they both wander the halls of the house alone, desperately searching but unable to find one another.'

'So when did you come here?' I asked, changing the subject. I didn't know enough about our existence yet to know for sure that there wasn't a possibility the story might be true.

Beth's face changed slightly.

'If you don't mind me asking...' I added, hoping that I hadn't upset her. It was hard to know the etiquette for such a situation.

'No,' she said, shaking her head slightly and looking at the floor. 'David and I came here a long time ago, I think. It was Henry who joined Mr Weatherby first. He managed to convince the old man that he needed company. I think Henry could convince anyone of anything. He's good like that. When he and Mary fell in love, she joined the family. It was Mary who found David and me. We had... passed,' she said, hesitating, 'because of a disease. I don't remember what happened, but we were trapped, completely alone. It was a horrid place. She said she could sense me crying. Mr Weatherby wasn't pleased, the thought of young people in the house, but he's warmed to us. We're quiet and don't cause any trouble. I don't leave the house except to go into the garden, but David sometimes goes out. I think he misses the outside world, seeing people. I'm quite content.'

I nodded. 'How old are you?' I asked her.

'I'm Fifteen,' she replied. 'David's eighteen, or there abouts.'

'Fifteen,' I mused. 'Shouldn't you have passed over then?'

Her face changed, she looked slightly pained.

'I'm sorry,' I cut in, worried that I had hurt her. 'I didn't mean to upset you; I just thought you might have been young enough, that's all.'

'I probably was,' she replied, her voice no more than a mutter. 'Mary thinks that I probably wanted to stay with David, that's why I'm still here.' She shrugged.

There was a lull in the conversation for a few moments; I was desperately trying to think of something that would lighten the mood.

'It's nice that you're still together,' I said. 'Mary says that doesn't happen often.'

'Yes,' she said, smiling. 'We have been lucky. We must have died close together. I don't know what happened to our parents, but at least we have one another.'

She stood looking into space for a time. I hoped I hadn't dragged up unhappy memories by asking her about her past life. 'What about Betsy?' I asked.

'Ah,' Beth said, smiling, 'she's lovely. She was the last to join us. I think she had been some kind of governess. She was used to spending her life with children. I know we're not exactly children anymore, but I think when Mary came across Betsy all on her own, she thought she would like to live with us. Be part of a family again.'

'Right,' I said, nodding. 'I thought she seemed like the mother of the group.'

'I suppose she is in a way,' Beth mused. 'I always think of Mary that way, but I suppose they both keep an eye on us.'

'You sound happy,' I muttered.

'I guess I am,' Beth said, chirpily. 'I've grown used to this life. You will too.'

'Can I see the kitchens?' I asked.

'Come,' she said, taking my hand once more.

We were now standing in a grand kitchen. Set in the centre of the main wall was an extremely large fireplace, with a large range placed in its hearth. There was an enormous butcher's block in the middle of the room and the other walls were lined with cupboards and worktops.

'I like this room,' I said, gazing around the place.

'Me too,' Beth said, 'even though it doesn't actually have any use for us now.'

'It feels as though it must have been the heart of the place once,' I mused, moving in a circle to take in every detail. 'I can imagine it when the house would have been alive. It would have had a roaring fire and staff bustling around making Mr Weatherby's meals.'

Beth giggled. 'Yes, that's a nice picture. It's funny to think of the house being dead too, I hadn't looked at it that way. It's kind of nice, in a strange way, to think that the house is just like us.'

'I think it is,' I said, smiling.

'Wait till you see this,' she said, taking my hand once more.

When I looked around we were now standing in a dusty attic space. 'Where's this?' I asked.

'It's the attic,' she said, smiling. 'I like it up here. There are lots of treasures hidden away. It's good fun to explore.'

I looked around, and gasped in amazement. The contrast between the brightly lit kitchen and the dark musty loft space was stark. Yet, despite the sparse light which was coming from a single tiny skylight at the far end of the vaulted room, I could make out every detail of the items surrounding me. My new world, it was a fascinating place where nothing was hidden.

The place did seem to be a bit of a maze, boxes piled up on top of one another as far as the eye could see.

'The space runs the full length of the house,' she said, skipping from one beam to the next. 'There are old paintings and books and all sorts of things. It's a great place to come if you're bored.'

'Doesn't Mr Weatherby mind people going through his things?' I asked. I had gotten the impression that the old man wasn't exactly thrilled at the thought of my arrival. I didn't want him to catch me nosing through his possessions.

'He doesn't really come up here,' she said. 'I think there are things stored up here that he would rather forget.' As she spoke, she motioned to a painting of a woman, half covered in a sheet.

'His wife?' I asked.

'No,' Beth mused. 'From what I can gather, I think this one was his daughter. I don't know the whole story, but it's something which makes him sad.'

'Right,' I replied. 'Well, I'll definitely need to fully explore up here.'

'Come,' she said, taking my hand. 'I'll show you to your room.'

I took her hand once more and found myself standing in a large room with a four poster bed in the centre. There were heavy red drapes hanging from the posts, although they were now moth eaten and dusty. I walked over to the corner and pulled a sheet which was over a dressing table in the corner. I struggled to get it to move. Beth walked over and pulled the sheet for me.

'Thank you, this is beautiful,' I said, smiling. I turned on the spot to take in the whole room. There was a large stained glass window with a seat built onto the ledge.

'I'm glad you like it,' Beth said. 'It's next to my room. I thought it might be nice for us to be close together. I haven't had a friend for a long time, well, unless you count David.'

'Brothers don't count,' I replied, smiling. 'Although, I'm not really an expert on the subject, I only have a sister.'

'Where is she?' Beth asked, genuinely interested.

'She's at home,' I replied. 'She's still alive.'

'Oh,' Beth replied, slightly surprised. 'You don't want to be with your family?'

'I...' I hesitated. 'It's not that. Things are just a bit difficult at the moment. I think they'd be better off without me hanging around. Mary says I should visit them, so it's not as if I won't see them anymore.'

'That's good,' Beth said.

It pleased me that she didn't want to pry further into my business. You didn't often meet people who were genuinely caring, without also wanting to get gossip from you.

'I'll give you some time,' she said, walking towards the door.

'You don't have to go,' I said, part of me wanting her to stay. 'I've been alone for such a long time.'

'Don't worry,' she said smiling. 'There's always someone around. Feel free to wander anywhere you like. Except, don't go into the room at the end of this corridor. It's Mr Weatherby's room, he likes his privacy.'

'I won't,' I replied. 'Thanks for the tour.'

'A pleasure,' she said. 'I think we're going to be friends.' Once she had spoken, I got the feeling that she was embarrassed, that she had opened up in a way she would normally not dare.

'I think we will too,' I said, hoping to reassure her.

She smiled and gave me a little nod. 'Have fun.'

She walked to the door and faded away as if into nothing. I sat down on the end of the bed, looking around my new bedroom. It bore no resemblance to where I had lived before. When I had first arrived in the house, it had all seemed very dark, but my eyes had carried on adjusting. I walked over to the dressing table and sat on the little bench which perched beneath it. I looked at myself in the mirror, the third time I had done that lately. It didn't look like me. When I saw my reflection I was slightly taken aback. There seemed to be a change in me. My hair seemed brighter and a hint of light seemed to have come back into my eyes. I couldn't be certain, but I thought that this light might mean I was happy.

Chapter Five
To The Manor Born

Time was once more passing very quickly and I found myself sitting in my room for a long while, strangely enjoying the solitude; something Mary had warned me would happen if I wasn't paying attention. I would need to watch that.

I had lain out on the bed and closed my eyes. I wasn't sure why, it wasn't as if my body needed sleep. When I opened them again, I saw that it was light outside. I rose and looked at myself in the mirror, smoothing my hair. It was then that I noticed what I was wearing. I obviously hadn't been thinking about my eternal afterlife when I had dressed on the morning of my death. It made me wonder what I had been doing that day. I was wearing an old pair of baggy jeans which had paint spatters on them and an ill-fitting sweater. To the others at the Manor I must have I looked like a vagrant. 'No wonder Betsy thought I was an urchin,' I muttered and sighed. There wasn't a lot I could do about it now.

'Hello, dear,' Betsy said, appearing behind me.

I started, momentarily scared that she had heard me talking to myself. I didn't want her to think that Beth and I had been eavesdropping on their conversation when I arrived.

'I hope you don't mind me stopping by,' she continued, smiling at me with genuine concern.

'No,' I replied, smiling. Her expression didn't suggest that she was there to scold me, 'not at all. It's lovely to see you again.'

She beamed once more. 'How are you settling in?'

'Fine,' I replied. 'Beth gave me the tour and left me to settle into my room.'

'Well, remember that you don't need to hide in here,' she said, kindly. 'Feel free to go anywhere you like. If you need anything, I'd be happy to help you.'

'Thank you,' I said, smiling at her. She was a genuinely lovely person.

'Are you happy here?' I asked. I didn't know why I felt the urge to ask her this question.

'Yes,' she replied, her response sounding measured. 'I believe so. I came here some time ago, but the place has a pleasant feel to it. I worked in plenty of houses when I was alive, but I think this one has the most relaxed atmosphere.'

'Do you know how you died?' I asked.

A strange look came over her face.

'I don't mean to pry,' I stuttered. 'I just don't remember anything about my own death. I suppose I'm curious about whether everyone else is the same.'

'Well,' she said, looking slightly flustered. 'It was an accident. I fell down a flight of stairs. One minute I was polishing the banister at the top of the staircase, the next I was at the bottom. The little rascal didn't mean it, but there we are.'

'Ah,' I said, not sure what to say next. 'I'm sorry.'

'Don't be, my dear,' she said, straightening her skirt. 'These things happen. I put my memory of events down to the agile nature of my mind. I always had to be organised, always meticulous. I think I knew immediately. Of course, I didn't leave the family straight away. I felt a sense of responsibility. Unfortunately, they left me. I don't know how long I was alone in the house, I sort of lost track of things. Then, dear Mary came along, such a wonderful creature. She brought me here.'

'That's nice,' I replied, smiling.

'Yes,' she mused. 'Things don't always work out the way we expect, but they tend to work out anyway. Now, I have to run along. Why don't you go for a wander, Beth will be around here somewhere.' She faded into nothing.

After sitting and thinking about what Betsy had told me, I decided that I would venture downstairs to see if Beth was around. I was desperate to remember what had happened to me, but sitting here alone wasn't going to do me any good. I could have stayed in my own house to do that.

When I appeared in the hall downstairs, Mr Weatherby materialised out of the lounge. He nodded to me grimly.

'Good morning,' I said politely. I wanted to do my best to show him that I wouldn't be any trouble. He grunted and carried on down the corridor into the library. I found myself feeling slightly disappointed. I had wanted to go into that room, but knew that the old man wouldn't want me following him in there. In truth, I wouldn't feel particularly comfortable sitting in a room alone with him either.

I headed for the kitchens. The room still seemed fascinating, and it was completely empty. Mary appeared behind me.

'Good morning,' she said brightly. 'Settling in?'

'Yes,' I replied, smiling. 'You have a lovely home here.'

'Well,' she said, crossing the room to stand beside me. 'Glad to hear you don't still think of it as an old wreck.'

I smiled bashfully. 'Sorry about that.'

'Don't be,' she said, smiling. 'You know, it can be your home too.'

'I thought I was just here to help during my adjustment period?' I asked, feeling hopeful that I could perhaps become part of the household.

'You make your own choices. I brought Betsy and Beth and her brother here. The difference was they didn't have anyone. You haven't lost your family, but it doesn't mean you can't join a new one.'

'Right,' I said, thoughtfully.

'What are you up to today?' she asked.

'I'm not sure,' I muttered. 'I was looking for Beth.'

'Okay,' she said, smiling at me. 'Henry and I will be around if you need anything.'

'Thanks,' I replied. She vanished from the kitchens and I stood there for a while looking out the window into the forest which lay beyond the grounds.

I decided to go out into the hall. It was then that I heard a sound coming from the music room. It was faint but clear, someone was playing the piano. It must have been Beth. I longed to go in, but remembered that she had seemed rather shy about people listening to her play. The music was beautiful, so I stood for a while at the door listening to the delicate melody drift out into the hallway. It had been a long time since I'd heard music; the sound made me rather emotional.

'She doesn't like it when people listen,' a voice said from behind me.

I turned quickly and saw that David was standing at the end of the hall, leaning against the banister with his arms folded. With his hair out of his eyes, his stare made me feel rather nervous; it was extremely intense.

'I'm sorry,' I stuttered, 'it just sounds so lovely. I didn't want to disturb her, so I thought I would listen from here.'

'Well,' he said grumpily. 'You probably shouldn't. She doesn't like an audience and I don't like her upset.'

'I didn't mean to…' I muttered.

He stared back at me.

I wanted desperately to change the subject. 'Was it you?' I asked, hoping that he would know I was talking about the day in the park.

'Was what me?' he asked, rather indignantly.

'I'm sorry,' I said, flustered. 'I thought I had seen you before. The first day I went out, I walked to our local park, I could have sworn that I saw you there.'

'You must have been mistaken,' he said shortly. 'There are a lot of us around.'

'Right,' I muttered, feeling rather stupid, even though I knew he was lying. I could never have forgotten the face I saw that day, it had been burned into my memory. 'I guess I'm just new at this. Where is this place?' I asked, trying to change the subject once more.

'What do you mean?' he asked.

'The house, where in the country is it?' I continued. This boy was very irritating. He knew exactly what I meant.

'You don't know?' he replied, mocking me. 'How can you not know where you are?'

'Well,' I said, feeling as though I was blushing, even though I knew I couldn't. 'When Mary brought me here, it was dark. We had been in my house in South London, but I don't know where we are now.'

'It's not particularly important,' he murmured. 'Once you're more used to this life, you'll find that geography doesn't really mean much. You only need maps if you're alive. We can go wherever we want to.'

'Do you know where it is?' I asked again, frustrated that he hadn't answered my question.

'Of course I do,' he snapped. 'It's in a village in Hertfordshire, somewhere. Northenshaw, or something. We don't go into the village. Mr Weatherby doesn't allow it.'

'Right,' I replied. This boy was becoming one of the most irritating people I had ever met. I also knew that he was lying, Beth had told me about the ghost stories. Regardless of what Mr Weatherby said, he had obviously gone into the village. I suddenly noticed that the music had stopped.

'Well,' he sighed. 'You've managed to disturb her. She's listening in to our conversation now.'

'How can you tell?' I whispered.

He shook his head, 'You really don't know a lot, do you...'

Beth appeared in the doorway. 'Don't be such a brute, David.'

'I don't know what you're talking about,' he said moodily. 'I was just making conversation. She was eavesdropping on you in the music room, I told her not to.'

Beth seemed to be blushing.

'It was lovely,' I added, trying to reassure her, 'and I didn't mean to intrude.'

She smiled meekly. 'Thank you.'

'What are you going to do next?' I asked her, hoping that she would spend some time with me. David had managed to irritate me and also make me feel rather uncomfortable.

'I don't know. Do you want to go to the library?' She suggested, looking delighted that I wanted us to do something together.

'Mr Weatherby's in there,' I said, quietly. 'I'm sure he wouldn't want to be disturbed.'

'Probably not,' she mused. 'I didn't show you the gardens when you arrived, they're beautiful.'

'Great!' I replied.

David shook his head and faded away.

'I don't think he likes me,' I said, taking her hand.

'Don't worry,' she said reassuringly. 'He just needs to get to know you.'

'Does he think I'm taking you away from him?' I asked. The last thing I wanted was to cause trouble between the two of them.

'No,' she said, smiling. 'We love one another, but he doesn't relish spending all his time with his little sister. I think that's why he goes out so much.'

'Where does he go?' I asked, wondering if Beth could confirm whether he often frequented London parks to stare at strangers.

'I don't really know,' she mused. 'He doesn't always tell me. He sometimes tells me stories that he hears, but I don't always know whether they're true or if he's just making fun. I think he enjoys going home sometimes.'

'Where was home for you?' I asked.

'London,' she said. 'We lived south of the river.'

'That's strange,' I said, 'so did I.'

'Really?' she said, smiling. 'That's funny isn't it? Who would have thought we would end up being friends.'

'I suppose we're not so far from London,' I said.

'I suppose not,' she replied. 'As I said last night, I don't ever leave the house.'

'Why not?' I asked.

'No particular reason,' she said, shrugging, but it seemed as if she was hiding something. 'When I was alive I spent most of my time at home. I had to help my mother with the house. This place is a palace in comparison. I tend to find enough things to keep me busy here and...' she trailed off.

'What?' I asked.

'I don't know,' she stuttered, 'I suppose I feel safe in the house. The things outside frighten me.'

'That's nice,' I mused.

She looked confused.

'I mean, it's nice that you're so content,' I said, qualifying my strange statement. 'Besides, they frighten me too.'

She nodded. 'You just need to learn to love where you are. I don't see the point in clinging to the past; all it does is remind you of what you've lost. Anyway, enough of all that, let's have some fun.' She squeezed my hand and we were standing outside to the rear of the house. The grounds looked enormous.

'Come,' she said, disappearing into the long grass.

I ran along behind her. The whole area was completely overgrown. Running through the grass was more like running through a jungle. Occasionally we passed by moss covered statues and fountains. It was a strange sensation, the grass quivered as we ran through, but it didn't really move. When I concentrated I could feel it, there was a light tickling sensation against my skin. As we ran, little rabbits fled on either side of us, scampering away from our presence in the garden. It was strange to think that the animals of the world were afraid of us; more aware of us than the humans who spent their lives surrounded by those long dead.

Beth stopped outside a big wooden door set in an eight foot high bricked wall which was coated in thick overgrown ivy. 'This is the best bit,' she said excitedly. 'I love the walled garden.'

It did look intriguing. As I gazed around, Beth skipped forward and disappeared through the heavy door.

I followed quickly behind her, looking forward to what waited beyond the giant wall. When I emerged on the other side, it was breathtaking. Spring obviously wasn't quite here yet, but the place looked remarkably green. There were large trees dotted around, and a beautiful pond in the centre of the garden. Beth was standing in the middle of a little bridge which spanned the water.

Without having to move, I found myself standing beside her. 'This is wonderful,' I said, smiling in spite of myself. I stood, instinctively taking in a great lungful of air, even though my lungs were redundant, it didn't seem to matter. I could feel my senses come to life as I took in the fresh air. Everything around us felt alive. The place felt completely filled with magic, bursting with life.

'It is isn't it,' she beamed.

I leaned over the wall of the little bridge to gaze down into the water beneath us. Amazingly, there were fish swimming through the water. The whole place seemed wondrous.

I gasped but Beth didn't seem to notice. I realised I couldn't see my reflection. It didn't make any sense when I knew that I could see my reflection in a mirror. 'Beth?' I asked.

'What's wrong,' she replied, looking concerned.

'Why can't I see my reflection?'

She leant over the bridge and I could see her reflection, although it did look faint. 'You're not concentrating enough,' she said. 'That and I think you've been alone too long.'

'What?' I asked, confused.

'You tend to fade a bit when you're unhappy or lonely,' she replied musingly. 'Your presence grows stronger when you are settled and happy, loved.'

'Right,' I mused. I screwed up my eyes in concentration and stared into the water. I thought I could make out my silhouette, but it was extremely faint. 'How come I can see it in a mirror?'

'I don't know,' Beth said, shrugging her shoulders. 'Maybe it's the light out here; it could be too bright for your eyes.'

'Hmm...' I felt frustrated. It didn't feel as though I would ever fully understand this strange life into which I had been thrown.

'Wait till you see this,' she said, gaily skipping over the bridge and down to the far end of the walled garden.

I followed along behind, feeling joyous. It wasn't hard to be happy around Beth. Simple things seemed to bring her pleasure, a gift which had eluded me since my childhood. It didn't make sense, but her joy was infectious. She vanished and reappeared ahead of me, sitting upon a swing. There were two of them side by side attached to a beautiful wrought iron frame. I giggled and ran to join her on the other swing. She had set the swing moving and it was swaying back and forth with ease. When I tried to get my swing to move, I had a little more difficulty. It took more effort for me to get it in motion. If I'm being honest, the swing was hardly moving at all.

'I love it here,' she said, shouting aloud as she swayed back and forth. I didn't remember the last time I had seen someone seem so alive.

I was busy concentrating on trying to get my swing to move more than a couple of inches; I might as well have been wading through mud.

She slowed to a stop and watched me. 'Don't force yourself too much,' she said. 'You'll get better at these things.'

'I hope so,' I muttered, my voice strained with effort.

'How are you settling in?' she asked.

'Everyone keeps asking me that,' I replied, shaking my head. 'I guess I'm doing okay. I do like it here, it's just hard, you know?'

'Yes,' she mused. 'I know it is at first. I have to ask. As you know, I don't get out of the house. Your style of dress is rather odd to me, is that what young ladies wear in your time?'

'No,' I said, bashfully. 'Well, yes, but not all the time. I don't know when I died. I wasn't exactly wearing my best clothes.'

'You're not stuck with them,' she said, smiling.

'What do you mean?' I asked.

'You can change them. Take my hair for example. One of my happiest memories is my mother braiding my hair. We didn't have a lot, but she said that I had the hair of a princess. She used to spend hours braiding it and pinning it up. So now, I always keep my hair this way. It makes me happy and in a sense, it keeps a little part of her with me.'

'I see,' I muttered. It made sense. I remembered the incident with the duffle coat and scarf. All I had done was thought about putting a coat on and it had appeared. I stood up from the swing and looked down at my body.

'Just concentrate on what you want to wear,' Beth said. 'Unfortunately, you can't really imagine yourself in things you didn't own. I tried that when I was new. Spent ages trying to change myself into beautiful dresses I could never have afforded when I was alive. It never worked. You need to be able to picture yourself in it. A lot of what we can do to change our appearance comes from our memories. I think that the way we appear physically is something that we project from within ourselves.'

I closed my eyes and tried to concentrate. At first I couldn't think what I wanted to wear. I hadn't exactly been the kind of person to set the fashion world alight. I then remembered a little winter skirt that I had owned. A grey woollen mini kilt, I had loved wearing it with a black shirt, black tights and some black boots. No heels, I'd never been able to master those, but this would at least make me look a little bit more feminine. I opened my eyes and looked down. It had worked.

'Very nice,' Beth said, clapping, 'although I don't know about showing so much of your legs. We didn't do that in my time either.'

I laughed. 'It's just fine in my time.' I did a little twirl. I hadn't felt this girly in a long while. Beth seemed to be bringing it out of me. I stopped part way through my spin with a gasp. David was standing at the far end of the garden, watching us. When he saw me stop, he disappeared. I went to sit back down on the swing next to Beth.

'Don't worry about him,' she said, sensing my embarrassment.

'He really doesn't like me,' I mumbled.

'I don't think that's the problem,' she said.

'What do you mean?' I asked.

'I haven't known him to be so interested in anyone in a long time,' she mused. 'I wouldn't be surprised if the problem with David was quite the opposite. Although, since I'm a hermit, I suppose I'm not exactly the expert.'

'Don't be silly,' I said, again, sure I would have been blushing if I were alive. 'I've never really had that problem before. I doubt I've suddenly become more interesting now that I'm dead.'

Beth sighed.

I looked up to see what was wrong and she motioned her hand up and down to my outfit. Without realising, I had reverted back to my baggy jeans and jumper. I shrugged my shoulders. 'I guess this is more me.'

'Don't put yourself down,' she said. 'Maybe you don't need to try to be so glamorous this time.'

I didn't rise from the swing, but closed my eyes and tried to focus again. When I opened my eyes, I was wearing a smarter pair of jeans and a nice shirt.

'Better,' she said, smiling. 'Although I thought only boys wore trousers.'

'Only in the dark ages,' I replied, laughing.

She pushed my shoulder and it set my swing in motion slightly. The two of us ended up laughing.

'Come on,' she said, standing up. 'Let's see if Mr Weatherby is finished in the library.'

'Okay,' I said getting up and reaching out to take her hand once more.

She didn't take my hand this time, but simply disappeared from the garden. I realised she was trying to make me do things for myself. I concentrated and found myself standing in the hallway outside the library door.

Beth was standing with her ear pressed against the wood.

'Is he in there?' I whispered.

'Not sure,' she said, her eyes screwed up in concentration.

'He's not there,' David said, standing behind us.

'Thanks,' Beth said, turning to face her brother. 'Do you want to come with us?'

'No,' he replied, indignantly. 'I'm not quite so hard up that I need to spend my time with girls.'

'Very well,' Beth said, sticking her tongue out at her brother.

'Finally decided on the outfit change I see,' he said to me. 'It's an improvement on your other look.'

I was sure he was insulting me again, but before I could respond I saw something, in the corner of my eye, move behind the boy. When I looked around him, I saw a small creature disappear into the kitchens. 'What was that?' I asked, completely taken aback. Whatever it had been, the creature was dead, just like us. Almost a tiny spark, it was gone before I had been able to see it properly.

'That's the cat,' Beth said smiling. 'I can't believe I forgot to mention him. We don't see him all the time, he tends to stay in Mr Weatherby's room, he's his cat, you see.'

'A dead cat?' I mused. 'So there are animals here with us too?'

'Not many,' David said, smiling at my obvious confusion.

This irritated me. He enjoyed the fact that I didn't understand half of what was going on. 'What does that mean?' I asked, putting my hands on my hips. I had never let a boy annoy me this much before, probably because I hadn't tended to make conversation with them in the first place.

'Some animals are here,' Beth said, sensing my frustration. 'If they were particularly attached to a human, they sometimes chose to stay with them. It tends to be dogs rather than cats. They form such strong ties with their owners. If a cat stays, it's a true bond. They are intelligent, you see, they don't tend to rely on humans. He must have really loved the old man to want to stay here with him.'

'So even though he wanted to be alone, his cat stayed behind for him. That's lovely,' I mused, smiling.

'Yes,' David said, with a mocking twinkle in his eye, 'it's very touching. You got a goldfish we should keep an eye out for?'

'What's his name?' I asked Beth, ignoring her brother.

'He's called Mr Fibbers,' Beth replied. 'He only spends time with us when he wants to, but he's funny. I enjoy his company.'

'Really?' I asked.

'By that,' David cut in, 'she doesn't mean that he tells funny jokes.'

'I got that,' I replied shortly. 'I'm not a complete idiot.'

'I'm going to reserve my judgement on that front,' he said, laughing to himself.

'What I meant,' Beth continued, 'is that cats are intelligent. I don't know what it is, but something about the plane we all exist on now, means that we can communicate with them more. Not conversations, but if you speak to him, he knows exactly what you're saying. I actually imagine that he would tell a good joke,' she mused. 'I think he spends most of the time chuckling at us anyway.'

'That sounds weird,' I mused. 'I can't imagine.'

'So, no imagination either?' David snorted.

'Come along, Portia,' Beth said, taking my hand. 'I'm sure David has to run along now.'

We were then standing in the library. 'What do you want to do?' I asked.

'Well,' she said smiling. 'I enjoy playing checkers, but if you think you would find it too hard, we don't need to.'

'Not you too,' I said, looking down. I still felt irritated by David. 'I know I don't understand a lot about this life, but I'm not a complete idiot.'

'I didn't mean that,' she said, smiling. 'I meant you might find it tiring trying to move the pieces.'

'Right,' I said, looking up from the floor. 'Sorry. I suppose, but it might be good practise for me.'

'Okay,' she said, moving across the room to where a gaming table stood. She began setting up the pieces. 'David prefers to play chess, but I think that's just because he loves to beat me. I prefer this.'

'Suits me,' I said, 'although it's been a while, I may need you to help me remember the rules.'

'Sure,' she said, sitting down on one of the chairs arranged at the table. She seemed pleased to have someone new to play with.

We had been playing for some time before I noticed that David was sitting in the opposite corner, watching us.

Beth winked at me when she saw me looking. 'Decided to join us after all?' she asked the thin air.

'I was bored,' he said. 'I didn't have a lot else to do.'

'You didn't fancy spying on people in the park?' I asked, irritated.

He didn't say anything and Beth looked up at me, confused.

'Never mind,' I said, looking back at the board, trying to figure out my next move.

I heard David giggle.

'What?' I asked, looking up, already on the defensive.

'Your face looks funny when you concentrate,' he said. 'It seems you're putting all your efforts into this one.'

'Yes,' I replied sarcastically. 'It takes both of my brain cells to figure out such a complicated game.'

He smiled. 'Well I won't distract you. I wouldn't want your brain to overheat from the stress.'

'We're trying to play, David,' Beth said, annoyed that her brother was interrupting us.

'Very well,' he said, rising from his chair and disappearing into thin air.

'That's better,' Beth said.

'Indeed,' I replied. Although, if I was being honest, I was a little disappointed that he had gone.

'Are you okay, Portia?' Beth asked.

'Yes. Why?' I asked.

'You've been staring into space for quite a while,' she said, a worried expression on her face.

'Sorry,' I replied, looking back at the board. 'I guess my mind wandered.'

'Hmm,' she replied. 'I won't ask where to.'

I smiled. I couldn't fool Beth. It's funny, you can spend your life feeling as though you've never had a real connection with anyone, and then a friend can appear out of nowhere. I had only known her for a short time, yet I felt we'd been friends for years. It had taken my death for me to make a true friend. *That's death*, I thought. God, I was starting to sound like Mary!

Chapter Six
Visiting Hour

I didn't know how quickly the days had been passing. I know that I felt quite content. Beth and I had become close and I couldn't imagine being anywhere else. We were lying out on the grass in the garden, the sun beating down upon us. It was early summer and I wished I could feel the heat of the sun upon my skin. It felt odd, being able to sense the light, see it upon my skin, but not feel the warmth from it. In this light, I didn't feel grey; it made me feel almost alive. The sunshine and happiness made me glow, on the inside at least.

'So,' Beth said, 'you're from London?'

'No,' I said. 'I did live there, but I'm not from there.'

'I didn't think you sounded like a Londoner,' she mused, sitting up on her elbows. 'Where are you from?'

'I was brought up in Whitby,' I said, smiling at the thought. 'Although, I'm not from there either, my mum is. I don't think I really come from anywhere. Dad moved around quite a bit with his work, but I lived in Whitby the longest; we stayed there until I was thirteen.'

'Why did you leave?' she asked. 'I can't imagine anything nicer than living by the seaside.'

'Like I said, my dad had to move around a lot for his work,' I replied. 'I can't say I was happy about it, but I didn't really have a great deal of choice. I think the move was probably why mum left. She had stuck it out for years, but after getting to go back to Whitby, she was never going to be happy in London. I know how she felt. I didn't really want to be there either.'

'What did you do in Whitby?' Beth asked, trying to steer me away such negative thoughts. She always seemed uncomfortable when I mentioned my mother. Perhaps it made her think of her own mother. 'Did you have many friends there?'

'Not really,' I answered. 'I've never had a lot of friends, for as long as I can remember, but I loved being there. It's the kind of place you could live forever on your own and not really mind. So much history, it made you feel part of something. Of course, I could be romanticising the whole thing. Maybe compared to London, my life there just seemed happier.'

'I think it sounds nice,' she said. 'Did you walk along the shore?'

'Sometimes,' I said, shrugging my shoulders. 'It could be busy in the summer. I liked climbing the steps to St Mary's Church. Then there's the Abbey, it's set out on a cliff.

She didn't look convinced.

'The church is lovely,' I continued, 'and you can sit among the graves and listen to the wind. It was reassuring somehow; you could almost feel the power of the sea in your bones.'

'It sounds as though you were made for this life,' Beth giggled. 'If you don't mind being alone.'

'Probably,' I said, smiling, 'but I don't think anyone really wants to be alone, you just get used to it. Somehow it becomes simpler than the alternative. Moving around is never easy; even though I was young when we came to Whitby, I think I always expected us to be dragged away. What's the point in making friends when you won't be able to keep them?'

Beth looked worried by my words; I could see what she was thinking. If I had been incapable of making friends in my living life, was I going to up and leave her now we were starting to become close?

'You know, if you do leave, maybe that's somewhere you could go? Whitby I mean... Mary said you were staying with us until you decided where you wanted to be?'

'I hadn't thought of that,' I mused. I understood what she was saying, even if she was too scared to actually ask me the question. 'I suppose so. Although Mary has said I don't have to leave. I can leave if I want to. I don't think I'm ready to be alone again, not yet.'

'I'm glad,' Beth said, seeming relatively reassured.

'Ahem.'

We both looked round and saw Mary standing, her arms folded across her chest. I also noticed that as we looked round, David, who had been lurking in the background, faded away.

'Hi, Mary,' I said, smiling. 'How are you?'

'I'm fine,' she replied, not returning my smile. 'Are you having fun?'

'Yes,' I replied, automatically lifting my hand to shield my eyes from the sun, I didn't actually know whether the action was necessary or purely habit. 'I feel quite happy here.'

'I'm glad,' she said, sternly. 'Do you remember what you told me the night I brought you to the manor?'

I looked at her, confused for a moment.

'You promised you would still visit your family,' she said, irritated that I seemed to have forgotten all about them.

'Ah...' I replied, 'that.'

'Yes, that,' she said, placing her hands on her hips. 'You haven't been to see them yet?'

'No,' I muttered, ashamed. 'I completely forgot. My time has been passing so happily here; you lose track, you know?'

'I'm glad, Portia, really I am,' Mary said, pleadingly, 'but you need to keep in touch with your family. I told you before; your time with them is short. I don't think you realise just how short; you only need to ask any of us, it's like you're squandering something we can't have. Besides, it means you don't know whether everything settled down after that night.'

I shuddered, I hadn't thought about that. 'You don't think?' I muttered, unable to finish my thought aloud.

'No,' she said. 'I don't think he'll have been back there, but you never know. You really should check. You owe them that much at least.'

'Do I need to go alone?' I asked her.

'I can't babysit you all the time, Portia,' Mary said, clearly trying to be patient with me. 'If you're going to adjust to this life, you need to learn to stand on your own two feet. If you get into any trouble, you can call on me, but I really think you ought to try going back there by yourself.'

'Yes,' I said, feeling slightly sick at the thought. 'I'll go.'

'When?' she asked.

'Today,' I replied, sounding like a moody teenager. 'I'll go today.'

'Make sure you do,' she said. 'I don't mean to be so cross with you, Portia, but this is important.'

'I know,' I muttered. 'I'm sorry, Mary.'

She smiled at me and faded from view. I could tell that she hadn't enjoyed being so harsh with me.

Beth took my hand and all of a sudden we were sitting on the swings at the bottom of the garden. 'You don't want to go home,' she asked, but in a way, it wasn't a question.

'I do,' I said, staring at the ground. 'It's just…'

'It's okay if you don't want to talk about it,' Beth said, setting her swing moving, 'believe me I understand…'

'No,' I sighed, 'it's okay. I had a bit of a rocky start to all this. There's nothing that bad about my past; except, I led this ghoul back to the house on my first outing. Mary saved me, but I'm scared to go back to the house in case he comes back. I know it's silly, I just don't want to make things any harder for my family than they have to be.'

We sat in silence for several minutes. The only sound was the squeaking of the metal swings we sat upon. I couldn't help but wonder about Beth's past, she was so secretive about it.

I was running over in my mind what I could ask her, nothing too probing, but the fact that we were talking about our families might mean she was ready to open up.

'David,' Beth called. This startled me and I completely lost my train of thought.

The boy appeared in front of us. 'What?' he asked, grumpily.

'Portia has to go and visit her family,' Beth said, 'and I think you should go with her.'

'Are you joking?' the boy asked, obviously not happy at the prospect.

My facial expression must have mirrored David's, but Beth was ignoring me.

'Mary won't go with her,' she continued, 'and she's frightened to go on her own.'

'Beth, don't,' I pleaded, not wanting to start a fight between the two of them. The last thing David needed was another reason to hate me.

'You're her friend,' the boy said, motioning to me as if I was a thing. 'Why don't you go with her?'

Beth's face changed. She was incredibly upset that her brother had spoken to that way. 'You know I can't leave the house.'

He sighed. 'I know. I'm sorry, Beth.' He paused for several seconds. 'I'll go, okay?' he muttered looking frustrated. 'When do we have to leave?'

'I don't want to put you out!' I snapped, unable to hide the irritation in my voice. I know Beth was just trying to help, but her brother was a complete nightmare. Even Mr Weatherby would have been a more suitable travelling companion.

'That's fine with me,' he said, holding his hands up. He began to fade.

'David!' Beth shouted after her vanishing brother.

The boy re-materialised.

'Be nice,' she said. 'Portia needs our help. For me...'

'Fine,' he said, holding out his hand for me to hold.

I hesitated.

'I'm sorry,' he said, although his voice didn't sound as though he meant it one little bit.

'Okay,' I said, turning to Beth. 'We won't be long. Thank you.'

'Take your time,' she said, smiling. I got the distinct impression that she was rather pleased at the prospect of her brother and me going off alone together.

She is off her rocker, I thought to myself. I knew she had some barmy notion that her brother had the *hots* for me, but the whole thing was completely ludicrous. I had never met anyone who irritated me more, and I'm pretty certain the feeling was mutual.

I shook my head at her, smiling at the dopey expression on her face. I then turned and reached out to take David's hand. As I did so I gasped, but we were gone.

'Where is this?' he asked, looking around himself. He had pulled his hand away and was examining it as though I had injured him in some way.

We were standing in the park again, right in front of the bench I had been sat upon when I saw David that day. It looked completely different in the warm sunlight; these new eyes showed me everything I hadn't noticed when I had been alive. I glanced ahead of me, to the spot where he had been standing the first time I saw him.

'Do you live in a park?' he asked sarcastically, looking around the place. 'I suppose you did look a little like a tramp when you arrived at the Manor.'

'I'm sorry,' I said, feeling that invisible blush once more. 'I was just a bit taken aback when I touched your hand.'

He looked at me for a moment. 'Yes, what was that?' he asked, interested in spite of himself.

'I don't know,' I replied, bewildered. 'It hasn't felt like that with anyone else, but I'm not the most experienced.'

'Me either,' he mused.

I stood looking at him for several moments. It had been extraordinary. As soon as our hands had met, I had felt a rush of heat going from my hand all the way up my arm. I could feel a temperature change, the first one since I had been afraid. The main difference was that this one felt pleasant. It made the sensation that Beth or Mary's hand gave me seem insignificant.

'Well?' he asked, waving his hand in front of my face. 'Is anyone home?'

I snapped from my reverie and looked at him. 'Sorry,' I replied.

'Shall we?' he asked.

I went to take his hand, but something made me hesitate and not for the same reason as last time. 'I want to ask you something,' I said.

'What?' he asked impatiently.

'Was it you, that day in the park?' I asked, watching him carefully for any reaction. I knew the truth; I just wanted him to admit it.

He stood silently for a couple of moments. 'Yes,' he muttered eventually.

'I knew it,' I replied, smiling. 'Why did you lie?'

'I don't know,' he said. 'It's not as though I was spying on you. I come here a lot. It was the nearest park to our house when we were alive. I just happened to see you sitting on the bench. You get a lot of dead people in a place like this. I guess I denied it because you made it sound like an accusation when you asked me.'

'Why did you go?' I asked, ignoring his lame excuse for lying to me. I knew I hadn't had any such tone in my voice when I had asked him about it back at the manor, I was only curious.

'I don't speak to strangers when I'm out here,' he said, motioning around the air. 'You never know who you're talking to.'

'I wish you had spoken to me,' I said, rubbing my forehead. 'If you had, I might not be in this mess. When I left here, the most horrible creature ended up following me home.'

'Sorry,' he apologised, for the first time his facial expression appearing genuine. 'Didn't Mary warn you about strangers when you met her?'

'Yes,' I said, frustrated, 'but it's a little harder in practice. Anyway, I didn't actually try to start a conversation with the man. He kind of approached me. I stood out like a sore thumb.'

He looked at me for several moments, his expression a picture of genuine sympathy. 'Let's get this over with,' he continued, reaching out for my hand once more. 'I'm sure everything will be fine and you can go back to visiting your family on your own in future.'

I smiled and took his hand, prepared for the heat this time. It was lovely, it felt right somehow. None of this made any sense. How could someone who irritated me so much evoke such a positive physical sensation?

This time I got it right, and we were standing in my living room. Time seemed to have changed around us, and it was dark outside. I wondered what could have caused this shift, but decided I should focus upon the task in hand. My father was sitting by the fire and I could hear Susan moving around upstairs.

'Well?' David asked, dropping my hand.

I felt a sadness wash over me as he let go of my hand. It was as though I had lost a shield of some sort, something that would keep me safe. 'I don't know,' I said, glancing around the room. 'Things look pretty normal; that's my dad.' I crossed the room and looked at him more closely. He looked even worse than he had before, drawn and tired.

I decided to check in on Susan to see how she was doing, David followed me. She was sitting on her bed with her headphones in, her eyes closed. I couldn't tell whether anything had changed and then I felt a great sense of cold wash over me.

'Not again,' Susan muttered. 'Please, Portia, leave us alone.' She removed her headphones and looked anxiously towards the window.

I felt a mixture of fear and confusion. Scared, I followed her gaze outside. He was there, at the window, peering in at us.

'Hello there,' he snarled at me. 'You decided to visit. I was thinking you'd never come back.'

'What have you been doing?' I asked, angry even through the fear that was mounting.

'Just checking in every now and then,' he said, shrugging his shoulders. The harsh tones of his voice made me shudder. With an animal-like whine, he placed his hands against the glass. 'I've been taking better care of them than you have! Abandoning your family, that's lovely that is.'

'Why can't you just leave us alone?' I begged, my heart silently racing once more.

'Where's the fun in that?' he asked, spitting at the window. 'I'm going to get in, whether you like it or not.'

'Who is this?' David asked. I could sense something like fear rising in him. This was bad, all we needed was an extra dose of terror around this creature.

'This is the *thing* that followed me home that day,' I said.

'There's no need to be insulting!' the creature spat, banging the window. 'What a way to talk about your friend. That's all I want to be, girlie.'

Susan whimpered at the sound.

I heard a thumping sound coming up the stairs and my dad was suddenly standing in the doorway. 'It's happening again?' he asked.

'Tell her to stop, Dad,' Susan pleaded, tears streaming down her face. 'I can't take this anymore. Please, just tell her to stop!'

'It's not her, Susan,' he barked, his voice hoarse.

I felt a sense of hope that at least my dad knew I couldn't be the one torturing them.

'It can't be her,' he continued. 'She wouldn't do this to us. Portia wouldn't…' his voice trailed off.

'Well who is it then?' Susan asked, exasperated.

'It doesn't have to be anyone!' he snapped at her. 'We don't know what this is. Whatever is going on isn't rational. We can't assume it's her.'

'Why can't we just leave,' she begged. 'Please,' she said, begging once more, 'please just let us leave, Dad. Perhaps if we got away…'

'You know we can't,' he replied, cutting her off.

'She's not coming back, Dad,' Susan snapped, bitterly.

He shot her an angry glance. 'Don't,' was all he said.

'You think I'm holding onto Portia? Well you're clinging onto someone else. Mum isn't coming back and we can't go on like this,' Susan shouted. She got up off her bed and fled the room.

My dad followed close behind her. 'Where are you going? Susan, don't!'

'No,' she yelled, 'I've had enough!' I could hear crashing and banging.

I appeared out in the hall and saw that Susan was in my room. She was throwing my things around and pulling my clothes out of the wardrobe.

'Leave us alone, Portia!' she yelled. 'We have to get rid of it, all of it!'

I stood in shock. I couldn't believe what was happening. For the first time since this had all begun, I was shaking. David put his arm around my shoulder. I felt the warm feeling come over me and it calmed me a little. 'What do I do?' I asked in a whisper.

'I don't know,' he replied, 'but I don't think you being here is helping things.'

'Please, Susan,' my dad was pleading. He marched into the room and stopped her destroying anything else.

For a moment she looked at him, full of rage and then buried her head in his chest, weeping.

'Come,' David said. 'I think you'll need some advice on this one. It's out of my league.'

'I can't leave them,' I said, feeling tears welling up.

'Portia,' he said, brushing the hair from my face. 'You can't fix this on your own. It could be your presence which is calling him back.' Warmth spread across my face where his hand had touched me. It was the closest thing to a proper blush I had felt for a long time; completely different to the invisible embarrassment I seemed to suffer from on a regular basis.

'Okay,' I said, closing my eyes and reaching for his hand. Suddenly the ghoul started pounding the window in my bedroom, yelling and shouting over at David and me. Fear gripped me once more as we left, even David's touch couldn't stop the cold feeling running down the back of my neck.

When I opened my eyes, we weren't back at the manor. It took me several moments to figure out where we were. I think it was the smell that helped me to understand what was happening.

'Where are we now?' David asked, looking around himself, bewildered.

'We're in Whitby,' I said, dropping his hand. It had been a mistake; removing the heat source made my legs buckle and I fell to the ground.

He knelt down next to me. 'Are you okay?'

'Yes,' I muttered. 'I'm sorry. Beth and I were talking earlier about my life here. This was a place I liked to be, a place I felt safe. I was completely terrified back there, I guess my screwed up internal navigation thought this meant we should be here.'

'Is this what I think it is?' he mused, looking curiously around the place.

'It's the graveyard of St Mary's Church, just along from the abbey. I used to enjoy coming here. Just sitting, listening to the sea.'

'You are strange,' he said, an amused smile forming upon his lips. It made his face look different, softer somehow. 'I don't know why anyone would want to hang around such a place at night.'

'I didn't tend to come at night,' I said, smiling in spite of myself and glancing around. 'My parents wouldn't have let me wander the cliff tops after dark.' I couldn't put my finger on it, but the words I had just spoken seemed to fill my stomach with dread. I shrugged it off.

'Right,' David said. 'Don't you think we should get home? It's a bit creepy here.'

'Creepy?' I remarked, smiling. 'You're a ghost, are you really supposed to be freaked out by graveyards?'

'I suppose not,' he replied, smiling once more. 'But put it this way, I wouldn't want to bump into the kind of spirits who hang around graveyards. Remember how well your last encounter went? If I were a creepy ghost, this is where I would lurk.'

'True,' I said, standing up and reaching out for his hand. 'I suppose you're probably right. Does that make me a creepy spirit?'

He hesitated before he took it. 'No,' he seemed to get the same relief from holding hands as I did, 'just an unusual one. I think I should be in charge this time. As fascinating as this little trip has been, I don't really want to see every place you've ever visited. Try to keep your mind clear.'

'Very funny,' I said, realising that I still felt a bit shaky.

He squeezed my hand and I closed my eyes.

When we arrived back, we were in the lounge. He sat me down on one of the couches and looked towards the ceiling.

'What's going on?' Mary asked, appearing in the living room.

'It's Portia's family,' David muttered.

'What do you mean?' Mary asked, looking at me. 'Did you go with her, David?'

'Yes,' he muttered.

'Why did you do that?' Mary snapped at him, furious. 'I told her to go on her own.'

'I think it was probably for the best that I did,' he replied defensively. 'Things are a little strange there.'

'It's him,' I muttered. 'He was there again. I think he's been haunting them. They looked ready to go mad.'

'I worried this might happen,' Mary said, pacing the room. 'You shouldn't have left it so long to go back. It's made it a game for him. If he can't have you, he'll drive them crazy. You should have called on me when you were there.'

'I'm sorry,' I said, a lump in my throat. 'I didn't know what to do. David said we should probably come home.'

'It's okay,' she said, sitting down beside me and putting an arm around me.

'What did you make of it, David?' she asked him, obviously wary of upsetting me further.

'He looked pretty menacing, but I'm not really an expert,' he replied, shrugging his shoulders. 'I didn't even want to go to the bloody place, but Beth made me.'

'Language,' Mary said, looking at him impatiently.

His words angered me. I had thought the two of us had made progress, obviously not. 'Well, I won't give you any trouble again, not unless I have any spying that needs doing. You needn't think I want your help.'

'Fine,' he snapped and disappeared from the room. The room was thick with emotion; I could sense his anger and frustration.

Mary sighed, 'That wasn't helpful, Portia.'

'I'm sorry,' I muttered. 'He just makes me so angry sometimes. I don't mean to.'

'Yes, well,' she said, 'I don't know what's been going on between the pair of you, but it doesn't seem as though he was the best person to have with you tonight. We need to focus on what we're going to do.'

'What are we going to do?' I asked.

'In all honesty,' she replied sighing once more, 'I don't know, but we'll think of something.'

Chapter Seven
To Bury Your Head

I skulked around my new home for the next few days. I wasn't aware of how many had passed; my melancholy seemed to be making everything merge. The seasons hadn't shifted around me again though, I suppose that was something.

I was avoiding Mary and I knew she wouldn't let me away with it for much longer. We needed to do something to help my family, but I was terrified at the thought of going back to my old house. I hadn't even seen much of Beth. The mixture of guilt and fear was making me stay away from all of them. I think she could sense that, so she kept her distance. Sometimes I felt rather bitter about how things had turned out with my living family. They had managed to ruin the only piece of happiness I had found for myself in a long time. These feelings came and went. I knew the situation they found themselves in was my fault, and from my last visit, it was obvious they were more miserable than I was.

Betsy had taken to appearing in my room and asking me questions. I know she was trying to help, but I didn't really feel like it. I tried not to be too short with her. She had been kind to me since my arrival and I had a funny feeling that Mary had been asking her to check in on me. I was glad that she wasn't doing it herself. I knew that she could feel my pain, it was part of her gift. She was obviously giving me a bit of space.

I decided to go for a wander up into the attic. I hadn't ventured up into the space since Beth had taken me on my tour of the manor. I hoped no-one would be up there. I was looking for something to distract me, and going through some of the treasures hidden up in the dusty old space seemed like a good place to start.

My ability to touch objects had greatly improved since I had arrived at the manor. It was no longer the strain it had been at first and I could open the drawers in my dressing table with ease. I hadn't played checkers with Beth lately, but I would probably be much better at playing games, maybe even moving the swing in the garden. The thought made me sad. The times when Beth and I had played together seemed such a long time ago, and something that I didn't deserve anymore.

I was as miserable as I had been in my old house, worse in fact; at least for a large portion of that time I hadn't been aware of my own predicament. Perhaps I would be better off there, sharing their misery, rather than hiding out in this place; constantly trying to avoid those around me, making them feel equally miserable.

I had settled down with an old photo album, looking through pictures of Mr Weatherby's family when David appeared in the room. I didn't need to turn round to see it was him, another sense that had been improving; although it only seemed to work with him and Beth, they were both so clear to me.

'You hiding up here?' he asked.

'No,' I replied shortly. I still didn't know why the sound of his voice filled me with irritation. Our relationship just didn't seem to make a great deal of sense to me.

'I think Beth is missing you,' he continued, keeping his distance from me in case I vanished.

'I'm sorry,' I sighed, feeling guilty. I didn't like the thought of hurting Beth. 'I've just been a bit down since all that stuff with my family. I wanted to be alone.'

'I understand,' he said, 'it was pretty scary.'

'Look, David,' I snapped, impatient, 'you don't usually make small talk with me. Is there something you want?'

'Just trying to be nice,' he muttered, I could sense that anger was rising in him too.

'Well,' I replied, 'there's no need to change the habits of a lifetime.'

'Why are you always so difficult?' he asked.

'Me?' I asked. 'You're the difficult one.'

He sighed. 'Look, I think you should speak to Mary, the quicker you get all this sorted out, the sooner things can go back to normal around here.'

'I wasn't aware that my presence here was normal,' I mumbled. 'I'm just a visitor am I not, an inconvenience?'

'Don't.'

I looked up, surprised. His tone was very different to the one I expected. Sounding strained, he was making a great deal of effort to be civil.

'I'm just trying to help you, Portia,' he said, looking at me with his strange, sad eyes. They seemed greyer somehow. They had lost some of their sparkle.

'I know,' I whispered, smiling weakly at him.

'Plus...' he continued, stepping forward slowly.

Here we go, I thought. I knew he must have had an ulterior motive for coming to see me. He wasn't usually this friendly.

'I can't stop thinking about that feeling with our hands,' he continued, looking down at his own as if they didn't belong to him.

'Oh,' I said, completely floored. I hadn't expected him to mention that. His words made me forget the anger I had been feeling. David had been kind to me on the day we had visited my family.

'That's never happened to me before,' he continued, looking rather sheepish. 'Well, with Beth I feel a sense of warmth, but never heat like that.'

'Me either,' I replied, mimicking the words he had used that first day we had held hands.

'It felt…' he smiled. 'I guess what I'm trying to say, is that I've missed you too since you've decided to become a hermit. Maybe we should try to be friends? I mean only if you…' he trailed off, looking rather embarrassed. He looked as though he was finding this whole experience rather difficult. It wasn't in his nature to make big speeches, making them to someone like me was obviously even more of an ordeal.

I looked at him for a moment, trying to figure out whether he was mocking me or not. He didn't break his intense stare, so I nodded.

His face broke out into a smile and he held out his hand, 'Come on.'

I rose from the floor and placed the photo album back on top of the box where it had been resting. I had been so consumed with my own problems lately, I hadn't really been thinking about David too much, but in mentioning the connection between us, he had made me yearn to feel it again; it was a physical ache. I couldn't believe that I hadn't felt it before. It was the closest thing to hunger I had experienced since starting this new life, but I hadn't realised this part of me needed *fed* until he held out his hand. I began to wonder whether keeping away from him had been adding to my unhappiness.

As I took his hand, I saw a new light in his eyes. Somehow they didn't look as sad as they usually did. He smiled briefly and squeezed my hand. I then realised we were standing in the lounge downstairs, still looking at one another. I was vaguely aware that the other members of the household were all gathered in the room as well, but they didn't seem to matter. Looking into his eyes, I could feel a warmth wash right through my body; as though I was standing slightly too close to the fire, but I didn't want to move away from the heat. In that moment, he didn't seem grey at all. His sharp blue eyes bore into mine and his pale skin seemed to glow next to his long dark hair.

Mary cleared her throat.

Beth was giggling.

'Can we get started, now that you have decided to join us, Portia?' she asked.

I snapped out of my daze and looked at Mary sheepishly, feeling extremely embarrassed. 'I'm sorry, Mary. I should have come to you sooner.'

Her face softened slightly. 'Don't be too hard on yourself, I know you're scared. I had a feeling that, David, here, might be able to drag you from your maudlin ways.'

I smiled. I didn't have the energy to argue the point with her, and I also didn't want to say anything rash that would jeopardise the fragile accord which David and I seemed to have reached. He had become strangely important to me, even if he still annoyed the hell out of me most of the time.

'Ahem.' This time Mr Weatherby was clearing his throat. 'Can we please get on with this?' He looked as though he was finding the whole situation rather boring and it made me uncomfortable. 'Some of us actually have things to do, Mary.'

'Of course,' Mary replied, not seeming at all disgruntled by the man's grumpy interruption.

I could tell from the expression on Betsy's face that she thought the old man had absolutely nothing to do.

It seemed our host found me extremely irritating. Perhaps this was just his normal disposition, I didn't really know. He was the only member of the household who had kept his distance since my arrival, something which had suited me until now. I could empathise; I didn't always like meeting new people and it was the old man's home after all.

'Portia,' Mary continued, addressing the group as a whole, 'has a ghoul who has been haunting her family. I think we need to do something about it, or Portia will never be able to move on.'

I found her choice of words strange, technically none of us would ever *move on*.

'You will all have noticed that her behaviour has taken a backward step of late. I think it would be unkind of us to not help her. After all, we were all new at this once.'

'A ghoul?' Mr Weatherby moaned. 'I rarely leave the house, young lady.'

Betsy snorted at his words; obviously he never left the house.

'What on earth makes you think I will make the trip to try to frighten off some ghastly ghoul?' He stared intently at Mary, completely ignoring Betsy.

'Because,' Mary continued, 'we all take care of one another. I'm sure that Portia would do the same for you.'

I looked at Mary, confused. I would have done anything for the people who had taken me in and given me a home, but I didn't tend to know what to do.

She continued. 'Anyway, I think the best first step is for us all to make a group visit. I don't know whether the creature will dare to appear with us all present, but if he does, I think we can chase him off. You know; strength in numbers.'

The group didn't look convinced.

'It's a good place to start,' Mary said, sighing.

'I'm game,' Henry replied, putting his arm around his wife and giving me a wide smile.

'Thank you, darling,' she replied, reaching up on her tiptoes to give him a kiss. Again, I noticed that they both seemed to glow slightly when they were touching one another.

'I'll gladly help,' Betsy said, touching her hair primly, 'anything to see this young lady smile again. We can't have you locking yourself away in your room, that's never good for anyone, dead or alive.' She shot a glance at Mr Weatherby. Obviously it was a bone of contention with her that he spent so much time sulking in his chamber. 'Besides, you were just starting to get a bit of light about you; we don't want that to fade away again.'

'I'm in,' David said, his voice sounding full of steely determination.

'I...' Beth stuttered. 'I don't know if I can. I'm so sorry...' she trailed off looking as though she wanted to cry.

'I know, Beth,' Mary said, smiling kindly. 'You don't need to come with us.'

'It's okay,' I said, smiling at her. 'I don't want you to do anything that frightens you. I know how that feels.'

'Thank you,' she replied. 'I can keep watch on the house,' she added hopefully. She wanted to contribute, even if she was too scared to come with us.

'Well,' Mr Weatherby grumbled, 'make sure you do.' He didn't look overjoyed that it was so easy for Beth to get out of making the journey. 'If this young girl is as much trouble as she seems we could end up bringing the bloody thing back with us.' If possible, he seemed even grumpier than before.

'Surely not!' Betsy exclaimed.

'No,' Mary chimed in. 'Portia hasn't done anything wrong here, Mr Weatherby. This thing latched onto her, but I can't see any reason for it to follow her here. It seems to have attached itself to her old home. Assuming it's still trying to gain entry to the property, we should be perfectly safe to enter and leave without it following us. Besides, it wouldn't have any interest in this place.

Ghouls prey upon the weak; I think being around somewhere like this would make such a creature rather uncomfortable.'

'Hmph,' the old man grumbled once more. 'I suppose I'll have to take your word for it.'

'Perhaps Mr Weatherby has a point,' Henry said.

Mary looked shocked.

'All I mean, love,' he said defensively, 'is that we don't know what's going to happen. Perhaps we should agree that when we leave, we don't come directly back here. We could even land somewhere near the village?'

'You know I don't want any of you going into that ghastly place,' Mr Weatherby said, obviously determined to disapprove of anyone's suggestions, even when they were agreeing with him.

'Good idea,' Mary said, ignoring the old man. 'If things go well, we can come directly home. If not, we can travel to the village square. That way, we can be sure we don't have any unwanted passengers before we come back here.'

'You should let Portia control our travel arrangements,' David said, a smirk on his face. 'We'd probably end up on a tour of the world.'

The group looked confused, and I felt mortified, an invisible blush rising to my face once more. He gave me a nudge to the ribs to show me he was joking.

'When do we leave?' David asked, changing the subject.

'I think it would be best to go as soon as possible,' Henry suggested. 'We need to make a visit to check things out. I don't know that this will work, but it's worth a try. Our presence alone may be enough to frighten the thing off for good.'

'Let's go,' David said, taking my hand. I felt the warmth coming from him, but could also sense some extra excitement. It was strange; he seemed a different person to the one I had met on that dark night when I had arrived at this place; although at times his moods seemed to change so quickly, I found it impossible to keep up.

'We shall all need to hold hands,' Mary said, reaching hers out towards Mr Weatherby. 'Portia has granted David and I access to her home, but we shall need to be joined for the rest of you to gain entry.'

Beth smiled over at me reassuringly; she seemed to be enjoying seeing David so happy. I smiled back and the room disappeared into blackness as David took us from the manor.

When we arrived at my house, the place was in darkness and everything seemed deathly still. David and I materialised first and Mary and the others appeared a few seconds later. I wondered if the delay was because of Mr Weatherby's reluctance to come on the journey.

'No-one's home,' Mary said in a whisper, looking around the place. 'Perhaps it's for the best. If we do end up in a confrontation with this thing, we don't want it scaring Portia's father and sister any more than they already are.'

I looked around the room. It seemed even stranger than it had on my last visit. Nothing had been cleaned in some time and there were bundles of newspapers lying next to my father's chair. There was a strange smell about the place, as though it was completely uncared for or even unlived-in.

'Are they still here?' Mr Weatherby asked, looking around the place, his nose raised in the air. 'The whole house seems dead to me.'

I looked at him, somehow terrified at the prospect, even though the same thought had run through my own mind moments before.

'No,' Mary said, sensing my unease. 'They haven't left. I can feel they have been here recently. Besides, all their belongings are here. There are few living people who leave such things behind.' She smiled at the man. He obviously thought that because he kept all his earthly belongings stowed away in a long dead house, that others did the same.

'How do you feel, Portia?' Henry asked, walking towards the kitchen.

'Fine,' I replied, my voice no more than a whisper, even though the others were now talking freely.

'There's no need to be so scared,' Mary said, touching my shoulder.

As she did so, David dropped my hand.

Mary turned away from us with a little smile forming around her lips. I wondered how far her special sensibilities went. Could she sense the warmth between us?

'Is he here?' Betsy asked, looking to the ceiling. 'I can't feel anything?'

'No,' Mary mused, 'neither can I. Perhaps he won't show himself when we are all present, most unfortunate. Portia, why don't you check all of the rooms before we go? We can wait for you here; there is no need to be afraid.'

I nodded silently.

Quickly I flitted from room to room in the house; they all appeared normal. Susan's room was strewn with clothes and school books, though my dad's room looked awful in a completely different way. There was nothing lying around, no photographs or personal belongings. The only sign that anyone stayed there at all was the messy unmade bed. I wondered how long it had looked like this. Had it been this way since my mum had left us? I deliberately left my own room to last, feeling a little nervous about what I might see on the other side of the door.

I stopped in the hall outside it and to my horror, noticed that they had placed a padlock on the outside of my room door. It looked hideous, harsh and industrial; the kind of thing you saw on a garage door. I then saw that there was a crucifix attached to the wooden frame surrounding the doorway. Did they think they had closed me inside the space, the evil spirit that was taunting them? I had to see inside, although I wasn't sure that I was ready for what would be waiting for me there.

When I arrived in my room I stood, shocked, for a moment. The place was a disaster. Somehow worse than before, they obviously hadn't tidied up the mess that Susan had left when I was last here. It was difficult to look at. I realised that in my state, I hadn't been breathing. I opened my mouth and took a deep breath to steady myself; as soon as the air hit my senses and flowed down into my unmoving lungs a great sense of nausea rushed through me. The smell was rancid; it was like rotten flesh and rubbish. What could be causing such a smell? I then felt a pounding in my head, my pulse appeared to be racing even though I didn't have one.

'Hello,' I heard, from the corner of the room. I quickly backed up against the far wall, peering through the dim light to see who had spoken. My developed senses for seeing in the dark seemed to have completely abandoned me in my terror.

The ghoul slowly moved forward and smiled when he saw that he had pinned me into a corner. The beast's features, which had already been vile, seemed to have worsened since our last encounter. His skin looked sallow and grey, more deteriorated than our normal deathly pallor. His teeth were yellowed and his hair even more filthy. His appearance as a whole made him look less than human.

'Glad you could join us,' he said, laughing. The stench of his breath crossed the small distance between us and made me cover my mouth with my hand to avoid being sick. A stupid human reaction, considering I knew I was incapable of such a thing.

He laughed at my response, it obviously showed my weakness. Even now, I was no better than the silly girl who stood waiting for the green man before crossing the road. I was a target.

'Help me,' I mouthed, no sound coming out.

In an instant, David appeared at my side. His eyes looked wild. Obviously he had been worried, waiting downstairs on my response. Mary materialised at my other side, Henry standing guard over her and scanning the room.

'Leave here!' Mary proclaimed, her voice strong and commanding.

'No!' the ghoul said, spitting at her.

Henry made to move towards him, but Mary held him back.

'You have no place in this home,' she continued. 'Leave these people in peace. You can't have her,' Mary pointed towards me.

'We'll see,' the ghoul replied.

'Everyone,' Henry said quietly.

Betsy and Mr Weatherby materialised in the room.

'There are six of us and one of you,' Henry said, fearless. 'I think you should move on, sir, lest you wish us make you?'

'How do you propose doing that?' the ghoul asked, giving Henry a mocking bow. 'Pistols at dawn? I can't see as you have any power over me. I'm just minding my own business. I think you should all leave. This is my place now.'

'They have pinned you in this room,' Mary said, unable to hide the disgust in her voice when she looked at the creature. 'What can you possibly gain from staying here? You can't get to her family and Portia has found a new place to live, you should leave.'

'They may have locked me in the room for now,' he said, grinning, 'but they'll let me in. I'll get the stupid little witch to open the door. She let me in the window after all. Despite her fear, she wants her darling sister back, that's all I'm giving her.'

'No you're not,' I said, my voice still shaky. 'Deep down, Susan knows you aren't me. You're just playing on her grief.'

'Gotta play to your strengths, beautiful,' he winked at me once more. 'Susan, Susan...' he said in his mock female voice. 'I whisper through the walls to her at night, loves that she does.'

David went to move forward, angered by the creature's words to me.

'David, please,' Betsy said, barring his way with her little hand.

'Yes,' the ghoul said, making a rude gesture at the boy. 'Why don't you keep your little brats in check?'

Betsy was obviously insulted by his statement, but she held her tongue. The creature wanted us to be angry.

'Portia,' Mary said, holding out her hand.

I took it gratefully, hoping that we were going to leave. However I noticed that she was holding Henry on the other side of her, and that the group seemed to be forming a circle, all holding hands. David took my hand, and I was scared to find that even the warmth from him couldn't banish the fear racing through my system. I could have been a block of ice.

Mary closed her eyes, and I noticed the others followed suit. I was too scared to close my eyes, too scared to leave us unprotected from the creature still lurking in the room.

While they stood there, concentrating, the creature began to dance around the circle. He was making rude gestures and noises at the group, none of whom took any notice. All except me.

'Portia,' Mary muttered, 'you need to join us properly.'

'I'm scared,' I whispered. The ghoul laughed when I said the words.

'He cannot touch you while you're linked with us,' Mary said reassuringly. 'This is a closed circle.'

'Okay,' I mouthed. I took a deep breath and tried to calm myself. I then closed my eyes and tried to block everything from my mind.

Suddenly, even through my closed eyelids, I could sense a light forming in the room. It was emanating from the centre of the circle and seemed to pulsate.

The ghoul screamed; a horrid blood curdling cry. He sped up his race around us and I could hear objects flying around the room, things being smashed against the walls.

My breathing started to speed once more.

'Keep it going, Portia,' Mary said, squeezing my hand. 'Don't let him reach you.'

I tried to put him from my mind. The light in the circle grew brighter and brighter until it felt as though I could actually see the room even though my eyes were closed. I could make out the people standing in the circle around me. Their shapes were lit up, glowing from the inside out.

All at once, there was complete silence and darkness.

'What's happened?' I asked, my voice, no more than a faint whisper. I daren't open my eyes, for fear that the creature had won, had broken the circle.

'He's gone,' Mary said, releasing my hand.

I opened my eyes. The room was destroyed, barely an item left untouched by the creature, but the foul smell in the room seemed to have lifted. I sighed.

'He's definitely gone?' I asked.

'For now,' Mary replied. 'Hopefully, he won't return.'

'Hopefully?' I asked, fear rising once more in me.

'You need to learn to control yourself, Portia,' Mary said, trying her best to not to sound short, but failing. 'It's that kind of raw emotion which attracts such creatures. When we were in that circle, he was joyous when he felt the terror that was coursing through you. It's what he lives for.'

'I'm sorry,' I said, putting my hand on David's shoulder, in the hope that the connection between us would give me some comfort. As I hoped, I felt a warm sensation wash over me.

'He probably won't come back,' Henry said, smiling at me.

'Yes,' Mary added. 'One of your family members obviously let him into this room. Luckily, they've managed to seal the door. He could return, but only to this space. It's probably not worth the bother, he would be as well moving on elsewhere to find a new victim. Still, you'll need to check in. It may be that we need to do this several times before he gets the message.'

I nodded, not sure if I dare speak.

'Humph,' Mr Weatherby grumbled, he obviously had no interest in making a return visit.

'Come along, Portia,' David said, taking my hand from his shoulder and holding it in his own. 'We had best get home, Beth will be worried sick.'

'Okay,' I said, smiling at him.

Chapter Eight
The Final Check-Up

It took me a while to get back to normal. While I had everyone in the house trying to reassure me that the whole episode was over, I couldn't quite bring myself to believe it. I didn't want to tempt fate. I still spent a great deal of time sitting alone in my room. I couldn't shake Mary's words from my mind. The ghoul may return and we may need to frighten him off again before he finally let go. I didn't know whether I could face him again. Every time I thought about it, I could almost smell his putrid stench in my nostrils. The sensation made me feel non-existent bile rise in my dead, dry throat.

Beth had been timid about approaching me since we got back, but I could sense that she was passing my room and pausing outside. As David had predicted, my senses had vastly improved. I wasn't great at detecting everyone in the household, but I could always tell if Beth or David was around me. She obviously wanted me to come out, but didn't want to pressure me into it.

'Are you coming down?' David asked, appearing at the end of my bed; he obviously wasn't as polite as his little sister.

'You know it's rude to enter a room without knocking?' I asked, unable to stop the smile forming upon my lips. It felt good to see him again, despite my melancholy.

'I know,' he said, grinning. 'I tried being polite, but you seemed to be ignoring me. I'm not a very patient person.'

'I haven't been ignoring you,' I said. 'Remember, I'm an idiot, I can never sense anything.'

'Sure,' he replied mockingly. 'Anyway, it's been ages. You couldn't expect me to be that patient.'

'Has it?' I asked. 'How long has it been exactly?'

'It's winter again,' he said, spinning round to face me and stretching his legs the length of the bed.

'Really?' I muttered. I needed to be more careful. Obviously sitting alone in your room was exactly the kind of pursuit that made time slip away from you.

'Beth is anxious to see you,' he said, nudging me with his foot.

'She's been around couple of times,' I replied, shrugging my shoulders.

'Yes,' he said, his voice mocking me once more, 'and didn't that tell you something? She must be desperate if she's creeping around outside your room.'

'Okay, okay,' I said, sitting up and stretching my arms and legs.

'Great,' he said, jumping from the bed. He stretched out his hand for me to hold.

'I think I can make it downstairs without your assistance,' I said, smiling.

'Stick then,' he said dropping his hand.

I smiled, then reached out and grabbed it anyway. 'You sure it's only Beth who's missed me?' I asked, jokingly.

'I...' he stuttered.

I didn't let him finish his sentence and before he realised, we were standing downstairs in the main hall.

He dropped my hand quickly. If we hadn't been dead, I would have sworn that he was blushing.

'You're back with us!' Beth said, appearing from the music room. 'How are you feeling?'

'I'm fine,' I said, beaming back at her. 'I'm sorry for being so moody.'

'Don't be silly,' she said, waving her hand dismissively. 'I don't leave the house at all, I can't judge you.'

'She doesn't leave her room,' David muttered mockingly, 'if you get to that stage, I'll be seriously worried.

Beth kicked him in the shins. 'Don't say such things. We don't want her disappearing back in there.'

David rubbed his shin, pretending it had really hurt him.

'I won't,' I said, glancing from one to the other. 'I can't afford to let more time slip away from me.' David seemed to have shaken me from my mood. While I couldn't say that I had forgotten my troubles, they didn't seem so bad when I was with them both. I would need to remember that in future.

'Come along,' Beth said, obviously in a jubilant mood. 'No-one's here.' She led the way to the library. 'Well, I say that; Mr Weatherby is upstairs, but he's been in there for days, he's not likely to disturb us.'

'Yes,' David said, stopping just outside the heavy wooden door. 'I'm surprised you and he aren't close friends, you both enjoy hiding in bedrooms so much.'

I reached out to slap his arm, but he had disappeared into the library.

We had been sitting in there for some time. The room felt cosy and safe. If it weren't for the fact that I couldn't feel heat, I could have sworn we were by a roaring fireplace. I think it was the company; they made me feel warm again.

I was watching Beth and David play chess when Mr Fibbers appeared through the doorway. He slunk across the room, his head held high and his tail swishing gently from side to side. A silver tiger in his living years, the grey hue of death suited him greatly. His piercing blue eyes definitely hadn't lost any of their lustre, and he stalked like a creature who knew he looked good.

'Hello,' Beth said, looking at the little creature as he padded across the floor.

'Meow,' the animal responded. It sounds crazy, but I could have sworn that the cat nodded its head in salutation.

'You haven't met Portia,' she continued, motioning towards me.

The cat crossed the floor and lightly jumped up onto the sofa next to me. He sat beside me and tilted his head on one side, studying me closely. His stare was unwavering, and for some weird reason, it made me feel slightly nervous.

'Hello,' I said, feeling a bit silly talking to a cat. 'It's a pleasure to meet you.'

He nodded his head.

'I know she looks a bit stupid,' David chimed in, 'but she's likable. Just don't ask her anything too complicated.'

'Ha, ha,' I said, throwing a cushion at his head. I was actually rather impressed with the ease with which I threw it; this wasn't something I would have been able to accomplish when I first arrived at the manor.

He ducked instinctively and it brushed a vase sitting on the window sill. We all sat still as stone as the vase wobbled on the sill, its movement unsettling a carpet of dust that covered the ledge. Luckily it steadied itself and didn't fall crashing to the ground. If we had broken it, Mr Weatherby would have been furious.

The cat made a curious noise, it resembled purring, but the rhythm also sounded like a deep laughter coming from his belly.

The sound broke the silence among us and we all ended up laughing.

'I think he likes you,' Beth said, smiling.

Mr Fibbers crawled onto my lap and curled up in a ball.

I sat for a moment, enjoying feeling the little moving weight upon my legs. It was rare to get such contact these days.

'He wants you to stroke him,' David said, not looking round in case it would break his concentration on the chess board.

'Right,' I said, lifting my hand gingerly and clapping the creature's head. As with the other spirits I had met, touching him felt just as solid as if I were touching a live animal. I could even sense a little warmth upon my lap where he rested. Perhaps I had found another friend.

He began to purr, a deep, strange, rhythmic thrumming. I could feel the vibrations pass through my whole body. Leaning my head against the sofa, I absentmindedly stroked the animal as he seemed to sleep, while David and Beth carried on with their game. This was the first time in a long while I had felt truly happy.

Beth glanced over. 'See,' she said looking at her brother.

Irritated, he looked up from the board and glanced in my direction.

'The light is back in her eyes,' she said, smiling.

I shook my head, feeling I had missed a silent conversation between the two of them.

'She's a simple creature,' David said, sighing, 'easy pleased.'

'I wonder where I can find another cushion,' I mumbled.

David chortled under his breath, his attention back on the game.

Several days passed in a similar manner and Mr Fibbers became a regular visitor among us. He seemed to enjoy the company. Mr Weatherby had taken to his chamber once more, and even the cat wasn't always welcome when the old man needed to be alone.

It was a dark mid-winter afternoon and Henry was playing chess with David to give Beth a break from being beaten. Mr Fibbers and I sat together; his place on my lap had become a daily routine for us both. Beth was sitting beside me on the large sofa on the opposite side of the room to the fireplace, humming a lilting tune to herself. Mary looked tiny as she sat in an enormous leather armchair by the fireplace reading a book.

'What are you reading, love?' Henry asked, content to look away from the game while David tried to figure out his next move. The dashing fellow never looked as if anything fazed him.

'Just musing over something,' she muttered, quite content, 'it's some poetry.'

'Why don't you read it aloud for us?' Beth asked. 'I would love to hear some poetry. It's been a while since I browsed through one of the books.'

'As you wish,' Mary said, smiling over at her. She cleared her throat before beginning. It seemed like a deliberate action to build tension.

'I sometimes dream about my life, in amber hues and reds.

Of afternoons in meadows green, of nights tucked up in bed.

I sometimes dream about my youth, of endless summer days.

Of warmth and love and endless hope spurred on by summer's rays.

Through every dream there is a thread, woven bright and new,
No matter where I dream I be, I always be with you.'

Beth sighed softly. 'I love that one.'
'It was beautiful,' I muttered. Mr Fibbers vibrated with agreement on my lap.
'Yes,' Mary mused. 'It is rather.'
'It's my lovely wife's voice that does it,' Henry said, gazing over at her.
'Oh, Henry,' Mary replied, 'don't gush.'
He winked in response and she giggled back at him.
'Who wrote it?' I asked, feeling slightly uncomfortable at breaking up their romantic moment. I hadn't paid a great deal of attention at school to poets and things, but just because I was dead, didn't mean I had to give up on my education. It's never too late to better yourself.
'It was Mr Weatherby,' Mary said, closing the book and holding it close to her chest, a gentle smile upon her lips. 'He wrote it for his wife. It's one in a specially bound collection, very romantic.'
'Really?' I asked.
'Yes,' Mary said. 'He wouldn't be pleased that I was reading it aloud, but I would imagine that he can't sense us at all just now. When he takes to his room, he's dead to the world.' She smiled.
I rolled my eyes at another example of her ridiculous word play. Mr Fibbers chortled. I seemed to have developed a bond with the little animal; he could sense my moods and reactions just as well as Beth or David.
I couldn't imagine Mr Weatherby being so eloquent, the old man rarely seemed to speak. 'He must have loved her very much,' I mused, trying to picture Mr Weatherby as a young man, frolicking through fields with a beautiful young woman. I couldn't do it. Every time, it just turned into Mr Weatherby as I saw him now, some random beauty at his side. As I concentrated, trying to think if I could remember seeing any pictures of him as a young

man in the attic, the image changed in my head. It was David and I running through the field. My eyes snapped open.

'Are you okay?' Beth asked, a look of genuine concern on her face.

'I'm fine,' I said, embarrassed. 'Just day dreaming.'

She giggled. Why did I always get the impression that she knew exactly what I was thinking? Surely *she* didn't have a gift she hadn't told me about? I looked at her, my head slightly to one side, scrutinising her delicate features to see if they gave anything away.

'What?' she asked, looking at me, confused.

'Nothing,' I said, shaking my head, 'just being silly.'

'Okay,' she said, exaggerating the word and nudging my arm.

'Don't act surprised, Beth,' David said, laughing. 'I told you she was daft.'

'Very good,' I muttered, laughing myself.

Mr Fibber's body thrummed on my lap, obviously amused by David's words.

'I don't mean to break up the fun,' Mary said, rising from her seat, stretching and crossing the room to sit across from Beth and I, 'but I think it may be time to pay your family another visit. I've been thinking about them for a few days now, you should probably check in.'

'Really?' I asked. I had been so happy. When I thought of my home, all I felt was fear.

'You need to be there for them, Portia,' Mary said kindly. 'We need to be sure that we have scared that thing off for good.'

'Do I need to go alone?' I asked.

'You should,' she said, 'but I won't make you. Remember we can always help you. All you need to do is call. You don't need us to be with you every time you leave the house.'

'I know,' I muttered. I knew she was right, but it didn't make things any easier.

'Check mate!' Henry cried from the corner, his face full of glee.

David looked annoyed as he leaned back in his chair, desperately scanning the board to figure out where he had gone wrong. He looked funny when he was irritated, his bright eyes screwed up and his brow furrowed.

'Don't be a bad sport, lad,' Henry said, rising from his chair and crossing the room to be with his wife.

'Fine,' David muttered. He was a terrible loser. He turned his chair round so he was facing us. 'I'll go with you if you want?'

'I'd like that,' I replied, smiling.

Henry whispered something to Mary, I couldn't make out what he had said, but she giggled and appeared rather sheepish when I looked round.

'What do you think?' I asked, wondering whether she would object.

'I think that sounds, lovely,' she replied, smiling. I had obviously amused her somehow.

'Well?' David said, holding out his hand.

'Sure,' I replied, lifting a grumpy Mr Fibbers from my lap and placing him on the carpet. The cat gave me an irritated glance and faded from the room.

'Just make sure you take us to the right place this time,' David said, smiling.

'What is that about?' Beth asked. 'You said something similar before. Where did she take you?'

'She likes to visit various places when she's out,' David said, grinning. 'The problem is that she doesn't know where she's going to land before she gets there.'

'That happened twice,' I cut in, slightly irritated by his exaggeration.

'Don't fret,' he remarked, taking my hand. 'I love the seaside.'

'You went to the seaside?' Beth asked, sounding slightly jealous.

'It wasn't that great,' he replied, smiling. 'We were in a graveyard on the side of a cliff at night, more spooky than picturesque.'

'Very good,' I said, squeezing his hand. 'See you guys soon.'

'Have fun,' Mary said with a wink.

Just as we vanished, I could have sworn I heard Henry, speak. 'Young love...

When we arrived at the house, I stood, embarrassed for a moment, unsure whether David had heard the words Henry had spoken, as I had. When I chanced a glance up at his face, it didn't show any sign of upset, irritation or embarrassment.

'Shouldn't you look around?' he asked, smiling at me innocently.

'Yes,' I uttered, looking away from his eyes. 'Sorry, I was slightly distracted.'

'Easily done,' he said giving my hand a squeeze. 'I know your little brain can only handle one task at a time. At least you managed to get us here first time.'

'Very funny,' I replied, sticking my tongue out at him.

Night had fallen and my dad was sitting by the fire in the cosy lamp-lit living room. A glass in his hand, he looked more agitated than usual. His expression put me on edge.

I could sense someone moving around upstairs, I couldn't be sure it was Susan. Something felt different.

As soon as I thought about it, David and I were standing in the centre of Susan's bedroom. She was in her usual spot on her bed; the only change, no headphones on. She too looked strangely anxious. The movement I could sense in the house was coming from another room, my room.

Dread crept over me once more. Ice water pouring down my spine, contrasted completely with the reassuring heat emanating from David's hand. 'Oh, no,' I muttered, creeping out into the hall, not letting David's hand fall. His warmth was the only thing keeping me from completely freaking out.

The room door was ajar and the light was on, there was someone inside, someone alive. Relief washed over me, but only for an instant. If it wasn't Susan or my Dad, who was in my room?

David gave my hand a squeeze. 'You should probably go in to check. Do you want me to come with you?'

'Yes,' I muttered, my voice reduced to a whisper once more. I didn't want to be alone.

I wasn't prepared for the scene that awaited me. The room was still in the same state of disarray as before, but standing in the middle of the floor was a priest, holding a bible aloft and spraying the room with holy water. He was the Polish priest from our local parish, Father Pach.

The man was speaking in Latin, so I couldn't understand the words he was chanting, but I could see the ghoul in the corner. He was hiding next to my chest of drawers trying to avoid the water as it splashed around the room, dousing the now filthy rubbish strewn surfaces.

The priest turned and a spray of holy water caught David and I square in the face. 'Oh,' I gasped as the water made contact. I could sense that David was also startled. It didn't hurt. It was actually a pleasant sensation, like feeling a warm breeze upon your skin. It gave me courage and strength.

'What's happening?' I whispered.

'I think they're trying their own methods to get rid of this pest,' David whispered, motioning to the creature cowering in the corner.

'Shut it,' he growled over at David. 'I won't take insults from a squirt like you, hear me?'

'Just leave,' I said, not feeling the usual fear I did in the creature's presence.

'I don't see why I should!' he snapped.

'What are you getting out of this?' I asked, holding his stare, something I hadn't been able to do before. 'Move onto some other poor sucker. You're wasting your time here.'

'Is that what you want?' he asked, an evil glint in his eye. 'If I go, I'm going with a bang missy, your choice.'

'Leave,' David said, trying to sound strong. I noticed that he was standing with his body almost in front of mine, protecting me from the ghoul.

'I'm quaking in my boots, little boy,' the ghoul said, mockingly. 'Trying to look big in front of your girlfriend are we?'

Suddenly he rose from his position on the floor and began to run around the walls. The whole thing looked completely unnatural. Gravity was obviously something else we weren't bound by. Before long, he was swirling around the ceiling, laughing a horrid evil laugh. The curtains began to billow and the light bulb hanging in the centre of the room began to swing violently from side to side.

The priest raised the volume of his chanting and continued to spray the room with holy water. Every so often the water caught the creature and seemed to burn his flesh.

Susan appeared in the doorway. 'What's happening?' she asked.

The priest didn't answer her, too busy trying to cast out the evil creature in residence.

'Dad!' she yelled. I heard him bounding up the stairs to see what was going on.

The ghoul built up to such a speed that he became a blur. In a flash, he was no longer circling the room, but had hurled himself at the priest standing in the centre of the floor. The Father was thrown from his feet and smashed into the wardrobe behind him.

'See you later, losers!' the ghoul cried. He flew through the window and the atmosphere in the room seemed to shift completely. It was as though someone had turned on a light or opened a window. There was a new freshness in the air.

For a moment I felt relief; he was gone. Then I remembered the priest lying on the floor at our feet.

'Father,' Susan cried, running towards the old man who was groaning and choking. Her voice threw the scene into sudden relief; this was an emergency.

'Are you okay?' she asked. 'Is it gone?'

'It is gone,' the old man muttered, 'but, please...' he cut off, his face turning red, his free hand clutched to his chest.

'What?' Susan asked. 'Dad, I think something's wrong with him.'

Dad had his mobile out and was calling an ambulance.

Susan cradled the priest's head in her lap and was trying to reassure him, but it was too late. The old man took one final rattling breath and was gone. She and dad seemed to freeze, both looking at the now still figure of the priest in front of them.

It was then that I noticed Father Pach was standing next to us, looking down upon his body. 'Hello,' he said calmly, smiling at David and me.

'Hello, Father,' I replied, not sure what else to say.

'How are you, Portia dear?' he asked.

'I'm fine, Father...' I stuttered. 'I'm so sorry about all this.'

'It comes to us all, my child,' he said, smiling gently.

'It wasn't me you know,' I said, worried that he would think I was the one who had hurt him.

'I know that, dear,' he said, smiling. 'I don't even know if the thing hurting your family was human. I told them it wouldn't be you.'

'Thank you,' I said, hoping they would maybe know now I wasn't the one tormenting them.

In an instant, the room had completely changed. I couldn't see Susan on the floor with Father Pach's body. I couldn't see my dad pacing around in the hall on his mobile phone, even though I knew they were there.

The room was filled with light. It felt like perfection, a warmth I hadn't felt properly since I had been alive, in fact, I doubted whether I had ever felt anything so joyous and pure. The closest I had come to such a feeling was when David and I held hands; it felt like liquid peace. The only figures I could make out were the priest, David and myself. We had become beings made of pure light; nothing grey, or dead about us. David was the most beautiful creature I had ever seen, a glowing angel by my side, his fierce blue eyes shining with a blinding ferocity.

'Come,' Father Pach said, holding out his hand. 'You don't belong here child; your family will be fine without you.'

'Father, I…' I stuttered. I was so tempted to reach out for his hand. I had never felt such longing. Surely this was what we all deserved. How could we be denied such a place? When I looked into the priest's eyes, nothing seemed more natural. Of course I should go with him.

'God will welcome you into his kingdom, Portia,' the priest said. 'David, you are his child too.'

'How do you know my name?' David asked, also feeling drawn in by the lure of the light before us.

'I know you,' the Priest replied. 'Why should I not know you?'

I glanced at David and saw the confusion in his eyes, the conflict. 'The light isn't for us,' I said, no conviction in my words.

'Of course it is,' Father Pach said, smiling at me.

'Portia, I think we should go home,' David said, shaking his head to clear it.

'I don't want to,' I said, taking a step forward toward the priest.

'Portia,' David said, in disbelief, 'what are you doing?'

I broke my link with David and began to step forward. In that instant, nothing but the love I could feel coming from the light mattered.

The Priest held out his hand, I reached forward. Just as my fingers were about to touch his, I felt David's touch behind me. In that moment I experienced the coldest chill as the light vanished, contrasting with the red hot touch of David's hand. Without my knowledge, or my consent we were dragged into blackness.

'Where are we?' I asked, panting. Had everything gone wrong? Where was the light? Nothing seemed to make any sense. I couldn't quite catch my breath, as though I had been dragged under water.

Panic coursed through me. Something had gone very wrong. We weren't supposed to go into the light, had we been sent somewhere else?

'We're home,' David said, taking me into his arms, 'in the garden. I thought you would want to compose yourself before we went inside.'

Confusion swept over me. Home, some part of my brain didn't seem to understand what he was talking about. Then reality kicked back in; it was a combination of disappointment and relief. We were home, that was better than the alternative.

'What happened?' I asked, allowing myself to fall into his embrace. 'How can we not deserve that, David? We should have been able to go with him. How can any loving God do this to us?'

'It didn't reject us, Portia,' he said, stroking my hair. 'I brought us home.'

I froze. 'You did what?'

He released me from his embrace, but kept hold of my hands. 'I brought us home,' he repeated.

I pulled my hands away violently. 'How could you do that?'

'We don't belong there, Portia,' he said, moving a hair from my face and searching my eyes for understanding. 'If we were meant to go there, it would have happened when we died.'

'How do you know?' I snapped angrily. 'That could have been our chance. Maybe we were supposed to go there, together.'

'I won't leave Beth,' he said, indignantly.

'What about me?' I asked, sheer fury building up inside me.

'You want me to choose between you and my family?' he asked, looking at me as though I were a complete stranger.

'Of course not,' I said, my voice still bitter. I felt-light headed, as though I was going to faint.

He looked at me for a long time, searching my eyes for something, I didn't know what. I looked back at him, my face a sheet of stone.

'I just thought…' he stuttered. 'I didn't think you would want to leave *us* either.'

His words didn't calm me. They should have, but they didn't. I didn't want to leave him or Beth behind, but I had never felt peace such as that which had come from the light. The absence of it was an unbearable ache in my still, cold, chest.

'I'm sorry…' he muttered. 'I didn't want to lose you. If that was selfish of me, then I'm sorry.'

'I… I…' I couldn't find the words. Closing my eyes, I vanished from sight. I didn't know where to go, but I couldn't stand there with him. It was as though my world had been torn in two. I had lost the chance to experience the peace I was destined for, and it had been taken from me by someone I loved. I hadn't realised until that moment, but I loved him. He was the most important thing in my existence. He was the person who gave me a taste of that peace, that warmth. How could I forgive him for taking away a chance at the real thing? I knew one thing, if I stayed in his company I would say things I'd regret, things that would cause irreparable damage.

Chapter Nine
Still As The Grave

I had no idea how long I had been sitting in one place. I couldn't sense anything around me, all was still and silent. Similar to the day in the park when I had first noticed David, it was as though the world around me had completely stopped. Someone had pressed pause on my existence. I hadn't even paid attention to my surroundings. It could have been six minutes or six years. David, the thought of that first day sent a stab of pain through my chest. I didn't know what I was doing, I longed to see him, but I knew that I couldn't move. I couldn't tell whether the sense of emptiness that filled me was because I hadn't seen him, or because I now knew the peace I was missing - the afterlife I should have had.

I was drawn from my thoughts of grief and loss by a spark of light in my peripheral vision.

I sighed to myself. If Mary was coming to scold me into coming home, I really wasn't in the mood. How had she found me?

I looked up. It was as if someone had turned the world back on, around me. I was huddled on the grass, leaning against a gravestone, once more, in Whitby. Of course it would be Whitby. It seemed to be the place I felt safest, more my home than London had ever been.

For an instant my thoughts turned to Havenshaw Manor, surely that had become my safe haven now? I shook my head; it hurt too much to think about my family there. I could hear the crash of the sea in the distance and the gulls hollering in the bay. The late afternoon graveyard was covered in snow, perhaps I hadn't been here for so long. It had been winter when David and I had made our fateful journey to visit my family, my living family. David. Thinking of him a stab of pain seared through my body, almost as bad as the pain I had felt when the light had vanished. My hand instinctively went to my chest, as though trying to plug a hole.

The person coming towards me was not Mary, or any other inhabitant of Havenshaw Manor, it was another ghost, a complete stranger.

For a second, I felt a rush of fear flood through my system. The last time I had spoken with a stranger, things had gone badly wrong. However, then I actually looked at the person approaching me. There was no malice or evil coming from her being. It was a woman in a flowing travelling cloak, the hood pulled up around her face. Something about her presence told me that she meant me no harm. I marvelled at the thought that I could now so easily tell when someone was good or evil. I may be a slow learner, but at least I learn from my mistakes.

'It's rather rude you know,' she said, her well-spoken voice rather stern somehow. It told me that she was not a young woman.

'Pardon me?' I asked, rather taken aback, and unsure to what she was referring.

'It's rude,' she repeated, lowering her hood gracefully to reveal her face. She was a middle aged lady with silver hair tied back in a platted bun, delicate curled wisps of hair framing her face. 'You shouldn't be sitting on someone's grave, unless it's your own of course. I know the living show us little respect these days, but we should at least have some common courtesy for one another.'

'Ah,' I said, getting up from the grass and instinctively wiping my trousers down. 'I'm sorry, I wasn't thinking.'

'You young people rarely do,' she said, stern once more. 'Who were you sitting on?' Something about her tone told me that she already knew the answer, but that she was going to drag out this telling off.

'Erm,' I muttered, turning round to peer at the gravestone in the gloom. 'A Mr Jonah Jinksworth, loving husband and father.'

'Ah,' she said dismissively, starting forward along the path once more, a faint smile upon her lips. 'He's an amiable fellow; you shan't be in any trouble. You should count yourself lucky. Some of us take it quite personally. If it had been Prudence Hopeworthy you would be in deep trouble.'

I stood and watched her as she carried on down the path. It was the strangest conversation I had ever had with anyone, living or dead.

Suddenly, she stopped in her tracks. 'Well?' she asked, peering round at me.

'I'm sorry,' I replied, unsure what I had done wrong now. I quickly looked around to make sure that I wasn't standing on someone else's grave.

She shook her head and tutted under her breath. 'Do come along,' she said shortly. 'We don't have all day.'

'Yes,' I replied, stuttering, 'of course.' I quickly walked up the path trying to catch up with her. Something about the way she spoke was so authoritative that I didn't hesitate to comply. She didn't wait for me to reach her and so as we continued our strange walk, I was always several paces behind.

'So who is Prudence Hopeworthy?' I asked, breaking the uncomfortable silence.

She stopped and I almost walked right into her back. 'Why, I am, my dear.'

'Ah,' I whispered. Was she leading me somewhere to reprimand me further?

'Come along,' she said, smiling for the first time. She obviously found my nervy disposition amusing.

'Where are we going?' I asked.

'I'll introduce you to the others. You can't stay out here forever, it's not healthy.'

'Right,' I said. 'How many of you are there?'

'There are four of us who reside here regularly,' she said, 'although we do have some drifters. You know how it is; people sometimes like to visit their graves.'

'I wouldn't know,' I muttered.

'What's that, dear?' she asked. 'You young ones do always mumble. In my day, our parents taught us to speak properly.'

'I'm reasonably new at all this,' I explained, making an effort to speak as clearly as possible. 'I don't know where I'm buried.'

'I see,' she said, nodding, her face looking compassionate for the first time. 'That does happen to a lot of people. You should be able to figure it out. Where are you from?'

'Nowhere really,' I said. 'Although I spent a good portion of my life here,' I motioned around the graveyard. 'But my family moved to London a few years back.'

'Ghastly place,' she said, with an expression as though she could smell something bad.

'Tell me about it,' I replied.

'You miss Whitby?' she asked.

'Yes,' I said sighing. 'I think that's why I ended up here. I was upset; I think I took myself to this place because it reminds me of happier times.'

We had reached a large mausoleum-like building. It could have been a chapel of sorts, I wasn't sure. She stopped at the door and motioned for me to enter. 'Whitby is in the blood, my dear. No matter where you go, all roads lead back to Whitby, even in death.'

I stepped through the door and found myself in a large, marble tomb. There was a little middle aged man sitting on a ledge in the far corner of the room, he looked as though he was smoking a pipe. This made me want to giggle. While he appeared to be puffing away on the thing protruding from his mouth, there was no smoke issuing from it. I wondered whether he was currently sitting on someone's grave, but decided not to ask. Prudence seemed to be warming to me and I didn't want her to think I was being cheeky.

Prudence had entered the crypt and strode past me towards the man. 'Jonah,' she said, her cloak vanishing and showing a long plain black dress. 'We have a stray. I thought I had best bring her in out of the cold. It'll be night soon and you know we sometimes get some unsavoury types around here at night.'

She turned to me. 'Some idiots seem to think it's funny to hang around a graveyard at night, so very childish. Even in death, there are those who would waste away their time being a nuisance to others.'

I nodded. I was suddenly grateful that she had brought me inside. I didn't want to meet the type of people that found that kind of pursuit amusing. They would probably be similar to my friend, the ghoul.

'I found her on a gravestone,' Prudence continued, turning back to the gentleman.

The old man chortled and lowered his ghostly pipe. 'Not a smart move, girly.'

'I know that now,' I said, smiling meekly at him as I walked towards where he was sitting. 'I'm Portia.'

'Lovely to meet you, Portia, such a pretty name,' he said, holding out his hand. 'I'm Jonah Jinksworth.'

'It's a pleasure,' I said, blushing as I realised who I was addressing.

'It was your grave she was on,' Prudence added with a slight shake of the head.

'Don't worry, my dear. I don't have any use for it,' he remarked, winking. 'It's much nicer to sit in here.'

Prudence muttered under her breath at the old man's response. She obviously didn't approve that he wasn't backing her stance on the matter.

'So you're a stray?' he asked, ignoring his friend.

'I guess so,' I said, thoughtfully. 'I have a home. In a way I have two. I just didn't want to be in either of them right now.' Somehow this made me feel idiotic. I had a choice of two places to live, and yet I always seemed to make things difficult for myself.

'With the living or the dead?' he asked.

'Jonah,' Prudence muttered, shaking her head. 'You do ask a lot of questions.'

'It's okay,' I replied. While I didn't tend to discuss this stuff very often, the man seemed genuine. I wanted to talk to him.

He nodded, and so I continued.

'I wasn't getting on too well with my living family, but I managed to find a lovely dead one to live with. Unfortunately, something happened, and I don't know if I can go back.'

'What?' Prudence asked, unable to help herself. Jonah pulled a face at her. She smiled at me apologetically.

'I was visiting my living family with one of my friends, David,' it felt strange to say his name aloud. Somehow it seemed a lifetime since it had last crossed my lips. 'We saw someone die. The man who died got to cross over. He was a priest who had known me in life and he asked me to go with him. My friend, David, dragged me away and I never got the chance. I just felt so… I don't know,' I stuttered. 'When we got home, I couldn't go in. I was so angry with him. I…' I trailed off.

'I see,' Prudence said. 'Seeing the light is extremely seductive.'

'You've seen it?' I asked.

'Yes,' she replied, her eyes now wistful, 'once. It was the most amazing experience.'

'Why didn't you go into it?' I asked.

'I didn't have a choice,' she said, shrugging her shoulders. 'The man passing over didn't know me. He didn't even see me standing near him. The whole thing was over so quickly, that it didn't enter my head to try. I was completely mesmerised by it; it was nothing and everything existing all at once.'

I nodded thoughtfully. It was such a hard feeling to describe, but somehow I knew exactly what she meant. Jonah looked mystified; it was obviously hard to understand how it felt when you hadn't experienced it yourself.

'How did you feel afterwards?' I asked, my hand instinctively reaching for my chest once more.

'I understand,' she said, putting an arm around me. 'It does leave you aching for its warmth. But, you must remember, we are not meant for the light. If we were, we would have crossed over when we died ourselves.'

'That's what David said,' I muttered, a hint of bitterness back in my voice.

'You don't like this, David?' Jonah asked.

'No,' I said, 'it's not that. I think that I... I don't know...'

'I think you do,' Jonah said knowingly. 'It sounds as though David couldn't let you go.'

'No,' I muttered. 'I don't think he could.'

'How would you have behaved in his position?' Prudence asked, now sitting beside Jonah and taking his hand.

It suddenly made sense. They were in love. I could see them glow slightly as they touched one another. It reminded me of the way Mary and Henry looked when they were together.

'I don't know how I would have reacted in the same situation,' I replied, although I did. I knew exactly how I would have felt. I would probably have reached out for him instinctively. Although he could have come with me, I thought bitterly. But I knew he couldn't leave Beth. I wouldn't have chosen to leave her behind. I suddenly felt a complete fool for hiding away.

'Has anyone been here looking for me?' I asked, looking at the floor, suddenly wishing to see them both once more.

'Him, you mean?' Jonah asked, a smile in his voice.

'I don't know, maybe, or anyone else?' I asked, trying to sound casual.

'I haven't seen any young men around the graveyard,' Prudence said.

'I don't get out so much,' Jonah added, shrugging his shoulders.

'Oh,' I muttered, disappointed.

'Don't worry,' Prudence said. 'Old Tom will be back soon, he may know something.'

'It's silly,' I shrugged my shoulders. 'I should go back, but I don't want to while I feel this way. I don't want to resent him for…'

'You can stay here for a while if you need some time,' Prudence said, sensing the conflict in my thoughts.

'Thank you,' I replied, smiling weakly. 'I think seeing Whitby again might be just what I need right now. Although I will need to go back, I can't leave them like this.'

'That's a good girl,' Jonah said, putting his pipe back in his mouth, an odd habit. I smiled once more, noticing that there was still no smoke emanating from it. He obviously carried it out of routine.

'Do you mind if I go for a walk?' I asked, with no idea how much time had passed since we had entered the tomb.

'Wait a moment,' Prudence said, walking to the door of the crypt and sticking her head outside. She pulled back and crossed the room back to Jonah. 'You feel free, it's daylight now. We don't get many strangers around these parts during the day, if you don't count the tourists. You should be safe.'

'Thanks,' I said, smiling and turning toward the door of the crypt.

They were being very kind to me, which meant a lot. Prudence kept her distance and only spoke to me when I approached her. I saw her watching me sometimes, but she didn't intrude upon my thoughts. It was nice having someone who understood, someone who had experienced the same thing, or almost the same thing.

'Do you think this feeling will ever go away?' I asked her one afternoon, looking out over the sea.

'It gets better,' she said, shrugging her shoulders. 'When I think of it, I still get that feeling in my chest. You know the one I mean.'

'Yes,' I muttered. 'I know the one you mean.'

'What you have to focus on is what you have, not what you're missing,' she said, touching my hand. 'If you had never witnessed that man crossing over, you could have carried on your existence here and been happy.'

'I know,' I said, closing my eyes and listening to the wind for several moments. 'It just all seems so, empty now.'

'Not empty,' she said, stroking my hair. 'It sounds as if you've found a nice home and people who care about you. There are plenty of people in the living world who never find such things.'

'Yes,' I replied, thinking about her words. I didn't think I had experienced such happiness when I was alive. Perhaps it was completely stupid to throw it all away over something I was never meant to have.

A big part of me longed to go home, to Havenshaw Manor that is. I definitely knew I couldn't go back to my living family right now. It would be like re-visiting the scene of the crime. The sight and smell of the place would just be an even bigger reminder of what I was missing out on.

I told myself I just needed a bit more time, although honestly I think there was more to it than that. I greatly enjoyed being back in Whitby. If I had met these people before I had David or Beth, this could have been a home for me. There was something else; it made me think about my mum, though not in a bad way. I started remembering things, long walks together, all four of us laughing. One afternoon, I had been staring out to sea and had actually travelled back. I didn't know how I did it, but it was just as it had been that night with Mary, so long ago. I was transported back to a day from my childhood. All four of us were out for the day. Susan and I running ahead along the beach, while mum and dad meandered along behind us holding hands. It felt happy, although a stab of pain had torn through me when I heard her voice.

'Don't go too far girls,' she shouted up the beach, her voice reaching us softly along the wind. That had been it. As soon as I heard that voice I was standing alone on the cliff again. I hadn't managed to visit a memory since; although I was still grateful it had happened. Being here was teaching me things about myself I hadn't realised.

Feeling as though I was back where I belonged had also helped me to focus my thoughts. For example, this whole thing had shown me how much I loved David. The last thing I wanted was to go back too soon and end up in a massive argument. I needed to come to terms with what I had seen, with what we were all being denied. I had long come to terms with the fact that I wasn't going to have the life I thought I deserved. There would be no change for me now, I would have none of the things I had taken for granted. No university, no career. If I couldn't have these, and I couldn't have the light, I wanted what Mary and Henry had, what Prudence and Jonah had. I had gone over in my mind what I would say to him when we met, finding dozens of different ways to try to settle things. We were always so volatile. At the same time, I knew he must feel the same. The heat we felt when we touched one another had to mean something. Didn't it?

At other times, my mind drifted from David. I didn't know if I would be able to let this fascination go. A futile part fantasized about being in the same position again, somehow being able to take them all with me. We all deserved it. There were times when I found my obsession galvanise into something else, something darker. At times I was determined to cross over, determined to find a way. When I felt like that, it was as if no-one heaven or earthbound was going to keep me out.

Chapter Ten
A Long Awaited Visit

I had lost focus upon time passing once more. I doubted I would ever get a handle on that. As soon as I lost my focus, the days just disappeared before me. Standing on the cliff's edge, looking to the eastern sea, my grief and loss were mingled with half finished, far-fetched plans about how I could find a way to take everyone I loved to the other side.

'What are you doing out here, girlie?' Old Tom asked.

The third member of Prudence's family, he was the only one who freely approached me. He didn't seem to register that I was moping around. In some ways, it was a good thing. He forced me out of myself, even when I didn't want him to. Maybe he understood more than I realised, but I guessed that the old man could never have had any daughters. He was a battered old fisherman who couldn't bear to be away from the sea. Were he to have his way, he would spend his afterlife working aboard a fishing vessel. He told me that he tried living on one for a while, but said that it somehow made him feel worse. Almost as though being able to see what his life had been without being able to have it back; that and finding it difficult to avoid the living men on the boat noticing his presence. It was such a confined space, that he ended up giving ships a bad reputation. Although, being a fisherman, he had always been a superstitious type; he said that even when alive, he had always had respect for the spirits that lived upon the sea. It just wasn't the afterlife for him.

His words had shaken me from my dark thoughts. 'Just watching the sea,' I said with a sigh. It still felt strange to me, that I could feel the breeze and smell it, yet the blustering sea air didn't move my hair or clothes. 'I love the sea here, but I wish I could feel it.'

'She is a ferocious mistress,' Old Tom said, with awe-filled eyes, 'and I know of your longing more than most. What I wouldn't give to feel the fresh sea air blowing through my hair.'

'Yes,' I replied, feeling more at home here than I had ever felt in London. The sprawling city had a presence that made you feel you were small, Whitby did the same thing, but in a different way. The power of the sea made you feel small, but rather than making you feel insignificant, it filled you with awe.

'Prudence tells me that you were hoping to hear from someone?' he asked.

'Not hoping,' I lied, 'more curious. I wondered whether any of my friends had been looking for me.' I didn't think my attempt at nonchalance hid my desperation very well.

'Right,' he said, showing no signs that he believed me. 'I have seen a young man,' he continued, deliberately avoiding eye contact.

'When?' I interrupted, willing it to have been David. All pretence dropped.

'A couple of days after you arrived,' he said, motioning to the gravestone where I had been sitting, huddled.

'Did you speak to him?' I asked, staring around at the grave as though it would make him appear before my eyes.

'No,' he replied. 'He watched you from a distance and seemed to be scanning the place looking for something. Whenever I tried to approach him, he faded from view.'

'He doesn't like strangers,' I muttered.

'Who does?' he asked, obviously trying to get me to open up.

'When did you see him last?' I asked, ignoring his question.

'It's been days now,' he said, shrugging his shoulders.

My face fell.

'That doesn't mean he's given up on you,' the old fisherman said reassuringly.

I nodded, but couldn't speak. I had hoped that David would guess this was where I was. I didn't like to think how detached I must have become to have missed his presence. He was the brightest spark in my existence these days.

As several more days passed Tom's news filled me with impatience. It made me want to see David again. I knew that the most obvious thing to do would be to go back myself. However, I couldn't leave until I decided what I was going to do. I paced the graveyard trying desperately to come up with a plan to cross over. I wouldn't be able to return until I had worked that out, or given up on the idea entirely. If I was going to attempt it, I knew he was bound to want to stop me.

I would then consider Prudence's words. I should try to be happy. If I had David, maybe I didn't need to cross over.

Every so often I would scan the churchyard for the face I longed to see; still this hope didn't stop my mind from meandering back to plotting and planning. Prudence and Jonah seemed to have taken to me, but I mentioned my dark thoughts to no-one. I had the impression that what I was considering was unheard of, or at least, was something that no-one I had encountered so far in my afterlife would understand. They accepted their existence here.

All I needed was the right person. The main problem was how to find the right person. How do you find dying people who were worthy of crossing over into heaven? The thought made me feel like a vulture. I didn't want to use people. Especially since the obvious answer, one I didn't want to consider, would be to find children. What monster would use children to get into heaven? The very idea made me feel sick to my stomach. Still, they were guaranteed entry.

I felt it. Everything else seemed to disappear for an instant. My plotting, the guilt I had been feeling, everything. It was the feeling I had been searching for. He was here. I hadn't needed to be looking around the graveyard. As soon as he appeared I could feel him, a searing bright light in my peripheral vision. It was as if the sun had come out. I spun around.

'Hello,' he said warily.

'Hello,' I mirrored, wondering whether he could see the guilt upon my face. Now I was looking at him, I did feel guilty. David wouldn't approve of what I had been contemplating. He couldn't possibly understand. At that moment I wasn't angry with him for dragging me away from the light, I was just so grateful to see his face. His long dark hair, almost covering his cautious deep blue eyes, he slowly moved forward. He looked greyer than I remembered.

'How are you?' he asked, his face carefully composed. He didn't want us to fight. I felt the same.

'I'm okay,' I said, shrugging my shoulders. 'I'm sorry I stayed away, I just wanted to take some time.'

'You don't owe us anything,' he said, his voice sounding strangely cold.

I looked up, my face showing the pain his words had made me feel. So perhaps I wasn't one of them. Maybe he didn't feel the same way I did. He had Beth, why would he need someone else? The lump in my throat, which had been excitement moments earlier, seemed to be choking me now. I knew I would cry if I tried to speak.

His face changed when he saw my expression. He looked horrified. 'Portia, I...' his voice trailed off.

I knew what he was trying to say. His face now told me that my doubts were completely unfounded. 'I've been thinking about you too,' I whispered. I couldn't speak properly. The overwhelming feelings that were rocketing through my system all felt so new to me. I think my ability to feel such passion had been nonexistent when I was alive; never having experienced such emotions made the whole situation so very confusing.

He smiled bashfully. 'It's as though it took what happened, your absence, to make me see,' he muttered.

'Yes,' I replied.

'I don't want to exist without you,' he continued, his blue eyes wary once more.

'Me either,' I said, wondering whether he could sense the hint of dishonesty in my tone. I tried to shake off the guilt. After all, my half-baked plan wasn't to leave David; it was to find a way to get us all in, to get us into heaven, where we belonged. Just because I wanted more, didn't mean that I didn't want him.

He stepped forward cautiously. I couldn't tell whether he was nervous or frightened. I noticed his hand, held out towards me. Not in an obvious way. It was more that his hand automatically reached for mine without his consent.

I didn't need to think about it. I wanted to feel his warmth too. I stepped forward.

As we touched, I felt a great sense of relief. We didn't look away from one another's eyes. In that moment, I found myself once again, having no care for my plotting and scheming. How could anything be more important than the way this felt?

'Will you come home?' he asked, his voice sounding slightly desperate.

'Yes,' I said, even though I had been set on staying in Whitby until I had decided what I was going to do. From the moment we had touched, I knew I didn't want to be separated from him again. This was why Mary had said that Henry didn't like it when she was away from him for too long. I had been putting the feeling in my chest down to my longing for the light, but it wasn't just that. The pain I felt inside seemed to be numbed by his touch. Almost an anaesthetic, David gave me a different type of peace.

He smiled. 'Thank you.'

I smiled back, unconsciously drawing forward to stand closer to him.

'Beth will be pleased,' he said, taking my other hand in his. 'She's been hounding me to try to make this right. I know she blames me, she's probably right.'

'I'm here because of me,' I said, trying to reassure him. 'Are the others angry?' I could guess that Mary wouldn't be happy at me running away like this. As one of her little projects, I imagined that I was giving her more problems than most. Considering she wasn't much older than me, she definitely knew more about life, or death I should say.

'Not angry,' he said, releasing one of my hands to brush a hair from my brow, 'just worried. Even old Weatherby asked about you, but he tried his best to make it sound that your being away was just another inconvenience. I don't think we realised how important you were to us. The house seems strangely quiet without you. Even if you did spend a lot of time hiding in your room.'

'I'm a moody teenager,' I replied, smiling. His words comforted me. They did want me there; it could be my permanent home if I chose it.

'Ah,' he said, smiling. 'We didn't have that luxury in my day. You went straight from being a boy to a man.'

'I'll need to ask you about that some time,' I remarked, realising that I knew very little about David's life. Beth had told me her story, but she didn't tell me a lot about David.

'Yes,' he muttered, his mind elsewhere. It made me worry about what he was going to say next, he was clearly nervous. 'Maybe we should go somewhere to talk before we go back. I think we need to figure a few things out.'

'That would be good,' I replied, feeling slightly anxious. I had never had this kind of relationship with a boy; I wouldn't know what to say. 'I'll need to say goodbye to the others here,' I muttered, stalling for time.

'Of course,' he said, releasing my hand.

'Come with me,' I added, disliking the lack of contact.

'I…' he stuttered.

'I know you don't like strangers,' I said, smiling, 'but they're lovely people. They've been very good to me.'

'Okay,' he muttered, looking rather uncomfortable.

We crossed the graveyard and headed towards the crypt where the other spirits lived. I didn't know if they were all there, but I was sure they would sense mine and David's presence once we got inside.

We were only in the darkened tomb a few moments when Prudence and Jonah arrived. Tom followed shortly after. I had never gotten to meet the fourth member of the family; a younger woman, Clara, she hadn't been around during my stay. Tom had told me she was a rather dramatic type and would often take to wandering the cliff tops, wailing.

'This must be David?' Prudence asked, smiling. It was funny to remember how stern she had been upon our first encounter. I now knew her to be one of the kindest people I had ever met.

'Yes,' I said, smiling. 'David, please meet Ms Prudence Hopeworthy and Mr Jonah Jinksworth.'

I heard Tom clearing his throat. 'This is Old Tom,' I said, motioning to the fisherman who lingered in the background.

'It's a pleasure to meet you,' David said, looking awkward.

'We knew you would come to fetch our little stray,' Prudence said, kindly.

'She does have a tendency to wander off,' David said, Prudence seeming to have disarmed him somewhat.

The room seemed brighter to me, I realised this was because I was glowing now too. David and I were beacons, making the dim crypt seem warmer somehow.

'You're here to fetch our girl home?' Jonah asked.

'Yes,' David replied.

'I wanted to thank you,' I said, smiling at them. 'I'm grateful that you took me in.'

'Somehow, I think we'll meet again,' Tom replied reassuringly.

'That's true,' Prudence said. 'As I told to you, all roads lead back to Whitby.'

'That they do,' I replied, suddenly feeling sad at the thought of leaving the place.

'Perhaps you could come and visit us sometime,' David said awkwardly, a long since used sense of social obligation springing to life in him.

'No, dear,' Prudence replied. 'We rarely leave Whitby, but thank you for the kind offer.'

'You may reconsider that,' I cut in, feeling that Prudence was refusing out of a sense of insecurity. 'We have a library full of books and a music room with a working piano.'

Prudence's face lit up at my words.

'And here you've been slumming it in a graveyard with us,' Jonah said, smiling. 'I don't know that Prudence can refuse an offer like that. She loves music, my Prudence.'

'Yes,' the lady murmured thoughtfully.

'Well, I'll come back and visit you some day,' I said, dropping David's hand and stepping forward to embrace her.

Jonah patted my shoulder and Old Tom doffed his cap.

'Good luck,' the old fisherman said.

'Thank you,' I replied, taking one last look at them.

With that we faded from the crypt. As we left I heard Prudence saying 'A piano…' I would definitely treat her to a visit to the Manor, assuming that Mr Weatherby didn't mind. It was strange, because I also knew that if I could persuade Beth, she would love a trip to the beach.

I had let David take charge and when we stopped, I felt confused. We weren't at Havenshaw Manor. 'What's happening?' I asked.

'As I said, I think we should probably sit and have a talk, just the two of us, before we go back.'

I felt my heart leap into my throat. I had forgotten his words back in the graveyard.

Of course we ended up in the park; the place where we first met, or saw one another at least. I don't think either of us wanted to have this conversation. Neither of us had a clue what we were doing. Once more, I lost track of time passing as we sat on the bench. Somehow I didn't want to speak; it felt like if we had this discussion, talked about the future, it would irrevocably alter everything. His presence gave me such physical relief; I didn't want anything to spoil it.

'So,' he said eventually.

'So…' I mirrored. So many of our conversations started the same way.

'I think I…' he stuttered.

'Me too,' I finished.

'Really?' he asked, his voice full of bashful relief.

'Yes,' I said, a pale non-existent blush crossing my face.

'This is all so new to me,' he apologised. 'I don't really know what we should be doing.'

'The story of my life, or death I should say,' I giggled. 'I don't know either.'

'Well,' he said, sighing, 'I don't know if that's helpful or not.'

I reached out and took his hand, hoping that the gesture would calm his nerves. I heard him take a sharp intake of breath as I touched him. 'I'm hoping we'll be able to figure it out,' I added.

He smiled at my words, seeming reassured. Then his expression changed, as though he remembered something awkward he had meant to say. 'Do you,' he stuttered once more, 'I mean…'

I didn't want to interrupt him this time. The whole situation was so strange. I wasn't really sure what he wanted to say. He looked so insecure. He had always seemed to self-assured to me, someone who mocked me for my lack of experience. Seeing him like this, I noticed that his brow furrowed when he was nervous, it looked different to when he was irritated. I wanted to do something to relax him. His beautiful blue eyes looked confused. For the first time, I noticed his lips. They were trembling slightly and I felt a strange new sensation.

'What I mean is,' he continued, suddenly blurting out the words at speed. 'I just need to know that you're okay with coming back. That you can forgive me for what happened that night; that you can forget about the light. I don't want you resenting me for what happened. I know I was selfish.'

I was flabbergasted. I don't know what I had been expecting, but it hadn't been for him talking about this. My head had been full of confusion about our changing relationship, not worrying about the light. 'David, I…'

'Look,' he said, obviously slightly worried by my reaction, 'I understand. I was there. I felt it too. I know that's why you stayed away.'

'I did,' I muttered. 'I've never felt anything quite like it. The closest comparison is the way I feel about you. The absence of that peace, when we left, was unbearable. I can't believe that we don't deserve that. That someone like Beth doesn't deserve that.'

'Don't think about it that way,' he said, looking at me warily. 'This is where we belong. It's where we were meant to be. I'm sure we can be happy enough at the Manor. Look at Mary and Henry, they're happy aren't they?'

'Yes,' I said wistfully. 'I just can't help thinking...' My voice trailed off. I had said too much.

'Thinking what?' he asked, his expression decidedly worried.

'Nothing,' I said, feeling rather panic stricken. I didn't want to get into this with him, not yet, not when I hadn't formed a proper plan. 'I've probably just been dwelling on it too much, you know?'

He squeezed my hand. 'Don't.' He lifted his free hand and slowly stroked my face. It was the most intimate gesture that had passed between us.

I blushed. 'What if there was a way...' I don't know why I said it. It slipped out accidentally. His touch had completely disarmed me somehow.

'What way?' he asked, moving his hand to my chin and raising my face so he could look directly into my eyes.

It was too late now. 'I...' I stuttered. 'I think if we were in a similar situation again, we could try crossing over. I don't see why all of us can't go. I got the feeling that it would have let us in. It was calling to us. That's the way things are supposed to be.'

His eyes hardened. 'I don't know that you're right. They changed the rules for a reason. What would happen to us if we got caught?'

'I don't know,' I said, feeling irritated. 'They'd probably just send us back here.'

'You don't know that,' he said, dropping my hand. 'There could be some terrible punishment for this.'

'You, don't know that!' I countered, suddenly angry. Yet again, we had ended up in an argument.

'Okay,' he said, anger in his voice now too. 'Neither of us know what would happen, which is exactly my point. What about Beth?'

'I think we should all go,' I said shrugging my shoulders.

'How do you see that working exactly?' he asked. 'She won't leave the house. Are we to start luring dying people to the Manor in the hope that they're not on the naughty list?'

'I don't know!' I replied, wringing my hands. I was stumped on that point. 'I... I had been thinking about children's hospital wards.'

'Please tell me you're joking,' he said, pain now in his voice. 'Portia, you can't use children for this, it's sick.'

I knew he was right. 'I'm not saying it's perfect. I need to think of a plan, I thought it might be worth a try.'

'What if you experiment with this and you can't get back?' he asked.

'I don't know,' I said, frustrated. 'I know it sounds selfish, but it could be wonderful. What if your mum and dad are there? What if Mr Weatherby's wife is there?'

He looked wistful for a moment, then re-focussed on me. 'I don't know that it's worth the risk. I don't want to lose you.'

'I don't want to lose you either,' I replied, reaching out and touching his face this time. I saw him glow faintly at the warmth of my caress.

'Look,' he said, leaning closer in. 'You need to realise, that's when I truly understood how I feel about you. I saw you step towards that priest: you were going to disappear from my world forever. I couldn't bear it. I don't want us to fight, I missed you.'

I smiled.

'Why don't we forget about this just now,' he continued. 'Maybe we can talk to the others and see what they think?'

'Maybe,' I said. I enjoyed the closeness, but I knew what his words meant. He was going to try to use the others to stop me. They would be able to bombard me with reasons why it was completely insane and I would give in, stop thinking about it.

Suddenly he reached in and gently kissed my lips. It was over in a split second, but the sensation was extraordinary. It was a moment of complete calm which seemed to jar in contrast with the startling warmth that I felt. Complete silence, highlighted only by the burning heat of his lips touching mine.

He pulled back from my face and glanced at me, looking for reassurance.

I smiled back and his face broke into a grin. The worry now gone from his brow, in that moment he was utterly beautiful. Not in the way he had been when I had first met him, not that strange sad beauty which had drawn my eye that day in the park. He had a look of pure happiness on his face, somehow more alive than he had been then.

'Sorry, it just seemed right,' he said, smiling.

'Yes,' I muttered, feeling completely distracted from the obstacles which still stood between us. His eyes were glowing. I wondered whether I looked the same. The grey seemed to have lifted from him somehow.

He leaned in and kissed me again, this time for longer. I didn't want the moment to end, as we kissed, he held me close to him. I had never felt such burning passion. The heat seemed to surge through my entire body; had I been remotely flammable I might have burst into flames.

Eventually he pulled away again once more and there was something else in his eyes, something wild. He smiled as he released me, I didn't think I had ever felt more joy, and he seemed to be feeling the same thing.

'Shall we go home?' I asked.

'Yes,' he said, standing up and holding his hand out towards me, 'lets.'

Instead of taking his hand, I folded myself into his arms and held him in a close embrace. Before I knew it, we were standing on the gravel outside the manor house.

Neither of us wanted to move. It felt wonderful, being surrounded by such warmth. After a few moments he unwound my arms and took my hand, leading me towards the house, still being careful not to completely break contact with me. 'Beth is going to be giddy.'

I smiled. The thought of seeing her made me feel excited. Perhaps life here wasn't so bad after all.

Chapter Eleven
The Grasshopper Who Sang All Summer

The summer months flew past. It was a happy time for me. David and I had continued to grow closer and the days seemed to disappear with me trying to split my time between either him or his sister. Of course the two often overlapped, but I tried to make sure I had time with them both individually. David spent most nights in my room and we talked, laughed and kissed the nights away; both feeling a new sense of hope in one another's arms. I was getting to know every part of him; his beautiful dark hair, his bright blue eyes and his intriguing smile. I never tired of making him smile. He no longer resembled the mysterious sad boy I had seen that first day in the park.

He rolled over on my bed leaning up on his elbows and kissed my nose playfully.

I giggled. 'How long have you been dead exactly?' I asked.

'Where's this coming from?' he mused.

'I'm just curious,' I replied, shrugging my shoulders. 'How much experience do you have on me.'

'I've been dead the best part of a century, give or take a few years, but experience? I don't think I have a lot of that.'

'What makes you say that?' I asked, now even more curious.

'I thought I knew stuff. I've explored the world a bit, you know, travelled around. But meeting you,' he sighed, 'nothing prepared me for this.'

I smiled. 'Glad I'm not the only newbie then.'

'Not at all,' he uttered, leaning down and kissing my lips, softly at first, then with more passion.

I wound my hands into his hair and took a deep breath as he moved down and kissed my neck. I could have melted there and then. Nothing had ever felt this good.

'So, travelling,' I muttered, a little breathless.

'You want to try travelling?' he asked.

'Maybe.'

'Well,' he said, laughing under his breath, 'I'm sure you'd be a natural.'

'Very funny,' I replied, now laughing myself. He was always having a dig at me and my unusual sense of direction.

We hadn't mentioned our conversation upon my return from Whitby and David was doing his best to keep me distracted. I wasn't going to forget about it, but I didn't want to spoil things and so let him continue for a while.

I don't think either of us wanted to dwell on something so negative. The endless days of sunshine had been an adventure for both of us. While we knew our feelings for one another were complete and unchangeable, we came from very different worlds, so to speak. David came from the late nineteenth century and saw himself as an adult. I knew that in most ways I also felt grown up, but I had experienced so little, and lost my life at a time when I was still trying to figure out who I was. Heck, I was still doing that, even in death. Something about the era David came from made him very certain about things.

It was a balmy summer evening, at least, I assume it was balmy. I couldn't feel the fading heat of the sun but as it went down, I could almost smell the heat in the air. David and I were sitting on the swings at the bottom of the walled garden, holding hands and swaying gently back and forth; the slight groan of the ropes the only sound between us.

As the light faded, it changed the way our strange eyes perceived things. If alive, my sight would have faded, but in death, it just adapted; not dissimilar to a night vision camera, only greyer.

'I love this time of year,' David said, in a whisper.

'Why?' I asked, peering into the gloom.

'It's a time that makes me feel special,' he said, smiling at me, as he looked at me through his hair.

'Why?' I asked again.

He laughed.

'What?' I asked.

'At least you didn't say why again,' he replied.

'Very good,' I said, smiling in spite of myself. 'I know... *here comes Portia with the inane questions...*'

'Your words,' he said, chortling.

'So, are you going to tell me?' I asked, moving my swing towards him and butting him on the shoulder.

He lifted his free hand to his shoulder pretending I had hurt him.

'Please?' I asked, trying to look demure.

He sighed and gave my hand a squeeze. 'It's just the way things look.' He glanced around the garden. 'Sometimes, it's easy to forget that we're dead, during the cold winter months, but, on a summer evening at dusk, when the bright colours of everything around us begin to change, it's like a gift. I feel like I can sense everything, everyone.' He took a deep breath, inhaling the smell of flowers on the light breeze.

'I've never thought of it like that before,' I said, wrinkling my nose. 'Although, I sometimes think you can sense more than is good for you.'

He glanced at me, confused by my words.

'Maybe I've just never accepted this life enough to see it the way you do,' I continued, feeling embarrassed. I had never spoken to David about how I perceived him; sometimes he was almost like Mary.

'I know you've had your issues,' he said, cautiously, 'but in many ways, my life here, now, is better than my living life ever was.'

'How so?' I asked, intrigued. While I felt that I had learned a lot about this strange, wonderful person, he didn't freely talk about his family. I didn't like to push the subject, I was sure he had his reasons.

'Well,' he said, thinking for a few moments, 'there isn't as much to worry about for one. When I was alive, my family had things pretty hard. My mother came from a relatively well-to-do family, but they cut her off after she married my father.'

'Was he poor?' I asked, curiosity getting the better of me.

'Financially,' David replied.

This made me even more intrigued. For some reason he seemed to need to share this, so I let him continue.

'He was a lawyer, but his own parents hadn't been particularly wealthy. My father always liked to help people, so even with his profession, he never tended to earn a great deal. I think my mother's family thought she could do a lot better, but they loved one another very much.'

'I think that's lovely,' I said, tracing one of my fingers along David's arm and gazing into the distance.

'Yes,' he replied, shivering slightly at my touch, 'but unfortunately love doesn't put food on the table. My mother tried to educate Beth and me as best she could, but as soon as I was old enough, I had to go out and try to bring in some money. My dad didn't like it, but what else could we do?'

'What did you do to earn money?' I asked.

'This and that,' he replied, shrugging his shoulders, 'whatever I could. Some jobs were better than others.'

Something in his face suggested that he had said too much. Whatever his past life had involved, I understood that it hadn't been pleasant. I moved from the swing and knelt before him in the long grass. Slowly, I moved the hair from his eyes and leaning in, kissed him softly on the lips.

He sighed. 'See…'

'See what?' I asked.

He chuckled, the moment of anguish now erased from his beautiful face. 'I meant, see, I couldn't imagine my life being any better than it is right now, with you.'

He tumbled from the swing and within moments we were both lying on the grass, my body atop his. He kissed me once more and this time held me close and tight to his body. I felt everything around us melt away, nothing mattered but the heat that pulsated through my system.

As he released me and we opened our eyes, I gasped; it was daylight.

David looked up at the sky and smiled as some little birds chirruped at one another, frolicking as they flew through the sky above. 'You're trouble you are,' he said, ruffling my hair. 'I've never met anyone so completely distracting.'

'Me?' I asked, laughing and standing up, dusting myself down.

He rose, grabbed my hand and we started walking towards the house. I didn't want this time to end. Everything that had gone wrong seemed a lifetime ago. Of course, it couldn't last.

It was a glorious afternoon and we were both in the long grass of the walled garden, while some way off, we could hear Beth singing to herself. The lilting refrain was the perfect companion to the mood I was in, everything around me seemed beautiful.

'What are you thinking?' David asked, rolling over onto his front so he could look into my eyes.

'Nothing much,' I replied wrinkling my nose. 'I'm just content. Although, I wish I could feel the heat of the sun, it still seems rather strange to me, not being able to physically feel the warmth.'

'We still have that,' David said, gently pushing a hair from my face. 'We just need to get it from one another.' He placed his hand on my cheek and I felt the burning heat from him flood through my body.

I giggled. 'True.'

He leaned in and kissed me, his long hair falling from behind his ear and covering us, blotting out the sunlight.

'Ahem,' Mary said, clearing her throat as she materialised behind us.

David pulled away and sat up crossing his legs. He didn't look embarrassed, instead he gave Mary a grin in welcome.

'Hey, Mary,' I said, rolling over onto my front and smiling up at her. Unlike David, I still felt slightly bashful at her catching us at such an intimate moment.

'Hello, you two,' she said, smiling. Mary found it difficult to hide her delight at the growing relationship between David and me. She was obviously as happy as I was to see him so changed. 'Portia,' she said, trying her best to look serious. 'Can I have a word?'

'Of course,' I said, getting up and dusting down my clothes.

David shook his head.

'Sorry, old habits and all that,' I uttered, shyly. I couldn't shake the impulse to make physical gestures that I would have done in my human body.

'Don't worry about it,' Mary said, 'I think it's important to hold onto your humanity.'

'Thank you,' I replied, sticking my tongue out at David as he chuckled under his breath.

'Shall we?' I asked Mary, motioning for her to walk and lead the way.

I could tell David was miffed at being left out and although he did his best to look disinterested, I knew his face too well.

'Portia,' Mary began, once she knew we were out of earshot of David, 'it's been wonderful having you back.'

'Thank you,' I said, smiling. 'It's great to be back.'

'You definitely bring David and Beth a great deal of joy,' she continued. 'It's nice to see them so happy.'

'I agree,' I sighed. 'They bring me to life too.'

'What happened to you was difficult,' Mary continued tentatively.

I felt myself freeze. What was she going to say?

'I know I always seem to harp on about this, but have you visited your family since it happened?' she asked, even though she knew the answer.

'No,' I muttered. 'I couldn't go back. I thought it would only remind me of how it felt. For David's sake, I've been trying not to think about it.'

'It's because of David and Beth I thought we should talk. You've found something special with them. When you left us, it really hurt them. I think you need to resolve this situation and choose a home; it's not fair on them.'

'One way or another,' I muttered, staring into the distance.

She looked frightened by my expression. She had obviously been hoping that I wasn't feeling so torn anymore.

'What do you suggest?' I asked.

'Perhaps visit your family again?' she enquired, still looking wary. 'It will allow you to check on how they've been doing as well as to see the place once more. You need to stop associating it with what happened.

I felt a pang of annoyance. It seemed as though no matter what happened or how I progressed, Mary was always scolding me and telling me to visit my family.

'Take David with you,' she added.

'Really?' I asked, momentarily taken aback. She always wanted me to be independent. Perhaps he was to play babysitter now.

Then it clicked. He was an insurance policy, the one thing that would make me want to come back. She was telling me I had to choose, but she was more or less trying to force me to realise that I belonged at the manor with them. This angered me, even though a part of me knew she was right. 'I think I can be trusted,' I replied shortly.

'That's just it, Portia,' Mary said, sounding yet again like the mature adult despite how close we were in age, 'I don't know that you can. Even you must admit that your behaviour has been a bit erratic since you came here.'

I glared at her.

'I know things haven't been easy,' she added defensively, holding her hands up, 'but I invited you here, I feel responsible. You need to make a choice, I won't see Beth and David so bereft again. It took them a long time to learn to be happy here, I don't want to risk them losing that.'

'I know you took me in,' I said, feeling a great sense of guilt wash over me. 'I don't want you to regret your decision.'

'Don't say that,' Mary said, looking as if she felt she had been too harsh, 'I didn't. From the way things are turning out, you were obviously destined for David. That kind of connection doesn't come along too often, in life or in death. I think our hearts only have room for one such love, something so powerful. The way you look at one another, it reminds me of how Henry looks at me, the way he makes me feel. Do you want to risk losing that?'

I nodded. I knew what she said was true. I had never experienced such a binding love, even with my family. It was bigger than both of us. Still, part of me wondered how glorious our love would be if we both crossed over. I gazed into the distance.

'Portia,' Mary said, using her freaky ability to read my thoughts using only the expression on my face, 'we don't know enough about heaven. Perhaps such love is our reward for staying here, our solace. Even in this perfect scenario of yours, would you relish sharing him?'

'What do you mean?' I asked.

'David's parents might be there, you might not have the same draw if he had the opportunity to have his parents back. Would you be willing to share him?'

'I...' I stuttered. 'Wait a minute. How do you know what I was...' I trailed off again, raw anger rising in me. I had only ever discussed my thoughts about crossing over with David.

'Portia,' Mary said desperately, 'before you go rushing off, remember what I said; visit your family.'

'That's your answer to everything,' I spat. 'I'm lost, what makes you think they can bring me home?'

I faded from view without looking at her and re-materialised in front of David.

'Hey you,' he said, smiling and getting up from the grass. His expression changed when he saw my face.

'Did you put her up to it?' I asked. 'Have you all been sitting talking about me? Poor, helpless Portia with her insane ideas...'

'No...' he looked completely panicked. 'I just want to help you. I didn't know what to do... I...'

I turned from him and marched several paces through the grass. As I turned around I saw Mary take shape beside him.

'Don't blame him, Portia,' she said sternly. 'He loves you, we all do.'

'I love him too,' I said angrily into the air.

'We haven't actually said that before,' he muttered.

'I know,' I replied, my voice quiet now. It seemed a ridiculous time to declare our feelings.

'You need to fix this, Portia,' Mary said, interrupting the moment between us. She looked sad, obviously feeling guilty at spoiling our happiness. 'There's something I think you should try. Do you trust me?' she asked. Something new had obviously just occurred to her.

I looked at her for several moments without answering. She was the one who had taken me from my home, given me a chance. I didn't like letting her down.

'Please,' David said, staring at me with a strange look in his eyes. It was desperation. I noticed that his hand was slightly extended; he was desperate for me to take it.

I looked back at Mary for a few moments. 'Okay, what are we going to try? Don't tell me, visit my family?' I said sarcastically.

'Not quite,' she replied. 'Your reaction has told me that you're beyond any comfort I thought they might bring you. I think that maybe it's time you know how you died,' she said matter-of-factly.

Chapter Twelve
Things Better Left Forgotten?

'What?' I exclaimed. 'Neither of you know how you died, what difference is it going to make to me?' I knew I sounded like a whiney teenager, but I couldn't help it and I didn't care. Mary always made me feel as if I was her project. Why would the answer to my problems lie in something she hadn't even experienced herself?

'I know,' David said nonchalantly.

'Excuse me?' I asked, feeling totally flabbergasted. A bolt from the blue, I had thought I knew him inside and out. As far as I was aware, Beth didn't know how she had died, though on thinking about it, it may just be that she didn't talk about it. David had never brought it up. Why hadn't he told me? A new wave of anger flashed through me. 'You remember it?'

'No,' he said, shrugging his shoulders, 'not exactly, but I went home to figure it out. I wanted to know what had happened to us. I was able to re-live some memories because I was back where it happened.'

'Why haven't you told me this before?' I asked bitterly.

'You didn't ask,' he said, shrugging his shoulders. 'Besides, it's not exactly an easy conversation to have. I don't like to mention it around Beth, she finds it upsetting.'

'Did it help you?' Mary asked, trying to get us back on topic.

'Yes,' he said musingly, 'it helped me to understand it all a little better. Although I didn't find mum and dad, it made me feel a little less alone in the world. I had hoped to see when they had passed, but it was beyond me. So are they, unfortunately.'

I couldn't believe that they were talking about this so calmly.

'What about you?' I said to Mary, still reeling from David's revelation. 'You don't know, do you?'

'I don't,' she said defensively, 'but I have also never felt the need, never felt so lost. My gift helped give me a purpose here and Henry has helped to ground me.'

David cast a downwards glance, was he hurt that he didn't seem to be enough to ground me? We had become so close; I couldn't understand why he hadn't shared this before.

'I don't know if I'm ready to find out,' I muttered. As I said the words, the anger seemed to ebb away; I was scared. 'How do you even do it?' I asked.

'I went to places I knew, places that would prompt memories,' David said, taking a tentative step towards me. 'You don't need to do it alone.'

'Is it the same as when you re-live a memory?' I asked.

'Yes,' David said, 'more or less.'

'Can you do that yet?' Mary asked.

'Once,' I muttered. 'In Whitby... it brought back certain memories for me. I don't know if I could do it again.'

'You can,' Mary said, smiling at me cautiously.

'If you can summon memories, why haven't you figured this out?' I asked.

'I don't know,' she replied. 'As I said, I don't think I've ever needed to.'

'And you think I do?' I asked.

'You need to do something, and I think it's worth a try, Portia,' Mary said, pleadingly. 'This is where we're supposed to be. Fair or not, you shouldn't be thinking the way you are. I think that trying this may help you find out who you really are, where you want to be. Maybe you need to know why you are this way so you can accept it.'

'That's the thing though, Mary,' I said, still full of frustration, 'it isn't fair is it?'

'You're right,' Mary continued, shrugging her shoulders, 'but that doesn't make what you're suggesting the answer. They must have thought about it, about people trying such a thing.'

'They,' I said, mockingly. 'They left us here! Why should we give a damn about what *they* think!'

'You have no idea what it would mean, even if it worked. What if your punishment for attempting such a violation was to be sent to the other place?' Mary looked completely frustrated.

'What other place?' I asked. 'Do you mean hell?' I couldn't hide the mocking tone in my voice.

'If that's what you want to call it,' she said defensively. 'I'm no expert on the subject, but I think it exists. It's why creatures like that ghoul of yours stay here, they're trying to avoid it.'

'He wasn't *my* ghoul,' I muttered.

'Portia,' David said, shaking his head.

'I'm sorry,' I replied defensively. 'I guess I'm just tired of being the problem child.'

'Well… Mary said, sighing.

'What?' I asked. 'Stop causing problems?'

'No-one's saying that, Portia,' David said desperately. 'I just don't want you to leave, is that so much to ask?'

'No,' I said, looking into his eyes. 'It's not.'

'Will you try?' Mary asked. She wasn't going to let it go.

I hesitated for several moments. I didn't know if I wanted to know what had happened. What if finding out made me even more miserable than I already was?

'Portia,' David said, taking another step towards me.

'Okay,' I muttered, closing my eyes as David took hold of my hand.

'Thank you,' Mary said. 'We will need to begin back at your home.'

'That isn't home,' I said, leaning my head on David's shoulder.

'Maybe so,' Mary replied, heartened by my words, 'but it's likely to be where it happened. I believe that a lot of people die at home.'

I hadn't thought of that; a sense of dread crept over me.

David took my hand and before I knew it, we were standing in my living room, Mary on the other side of David. My long dead heart should have been pounding in my chest; I couldn't remember feeling more nervous.

The house felt empty, as it always seemed to be, although something was definitely different.

'This place is changed,' Mary said, glancing around the room. 'The whole place seems so much brighter.'

'Yes,' David replied, squeezing my hand. 'I think that now the ghoul has gone, it has helped your family to move on from their grief.'

'Great,' I muttered, my voice barely a whisper.

'It's a good thing, Portia,' Mary said, smiling at me. 'It might help you let go of your own.'

'Grief?' I asked. I hadn't been aware that I was grieving.

'Yes,' Mary replied, shrugging her shoulders, 'in a sense. When I met you, you were grieving for the life you had lost, for the mother who had abandoned you. Since then, you have found some happiness, but then you have seen the peace that we are all denied. So now, you grieve for the loss of what you think your afterlife should have been.'

'Right,' I muttered. What she said made sense, but it was still hard to hear. 'Where do we start?'

'I'm not sure,' Mary replied. 'Why don't we try your room?'

I felt a lump in my throat, the room where it had all happened. David sensed my tension and squeezed my hand reassuringly. I focussed on his warmth passing through me and it helped, a little.

'Come,' Mary said, and took his hand on the other side. She was obviously going to take us to my room, whether I liked it or not.

We were there. I almost gasped as I looked around. The room couldn't have been more different. The last time we had been there, the place had been a complete mess, my things strewn all over the floor. As I remembered, I could almost taste the foul stench caused by the hideous ghoul that had taken up residence in the space.

Suddenly my memory changed. I felt I could almost sense the light around me; see the old priest's face willing me to go with him. Allowing a sense of desperation to overwhelm me, without meaning too, I accidentally transported us all back to that moment in time. All three of us stood, still as stone, mesmerised by the peace emanating from the glowing portal before us.

'Portia,' Mary muttered, her voice strained, 'this isn't helping. Please…'

David grabbed me and forced me into his arms, placing my head on his shoulder. As he did so, the scene faded and we found ourselves standing once more in my empty bedroom, as quiet as it had been when we arrived. In that instant, I felt that gaping hole in my chest. The loss of being taken away from that love, the place I thought I deserved.

'I had no idea it was quite so alluring,' Mary said, looking at me with a strange expression on her face. I think she finally realised why I had been so completely bereft when this had happened. Everything felt slightly colder and emptier now that the light had gone. Even the replica of the event my mind had conjured had been intoxicating.

'It was incredibly hard to resist,' David told her.

I hadn't thought about David. I hadn't even considered how he must have really struggled to walk away from the light that night. His love for his sister was strong enough that he could resist such blissful peace. His love for me was strong enough that he would risk breaking our then fragile relationship rather then let me leave his world behind.

'I'm sorry,' I muttered, lifting my head from his shoulder.

'It's fine,' he said, smiling weakly. 'I figured it was inevitable. We just need to focus on what we're here for now.' He brushed my hair from my eyes and stroked my cheek. 'We can do this.'

'Okay,' I said, unfolding myself from his arms. 'Mary, I'm sorry about that. I'll focus myself now.'

'Well done,' Mary replied. She wasn't as scolding as usual. I presume letting her see what we had experienced had changed how she viewed my behaviour of late.

'So what now?' David asked.

'Look around you,' Mary replied.

I stared around the room for several minutes. The place looked vastly improved since my last visit, but it had also changed in other ways. Most of my stuff had been removed from the room and it appeared to be set up more like a guest room. There was a photograph of me and the rest of the family on a bedside cabinet, but other than that it didn't resemble *my* room at all.

'It's too different,' I muttered.

'It does seem that your family has chosen to re-decorate,' Mary said, walking over to the bedside cabinet and looking at the picture in a frame. 'It's probably a good thing, all part of the healing process.'

'Yes,' I said, feeling slightly hurt by the room which seemed to hold no part of me anymore. 'I don't know if this place will help me though, it all seems too foreign. It's as though they've forgotten me altogether.'

'Not altogether,' Mary said, motioning to the photo sitting by the bed. 'All of your family I presume. Your mother was an attractive woman.'

'You look so alike,' David said, looking at the photo wistfully.

'My mother...' my voice trailed off. I hadn't paid a great deal of attention to the picture when I had scanned the room, but there she was. 'I thought my dad had gotten rid of all the pictures of her,' I continued, slowly stepping forward.

'Not all of them it seems,' Mary said, smiling at me demurely.

I knelt down in front of the bedside cabinet and examined the picture; I didn't know whether I would have the strength to pick it up. The whole thing was so unnerving.

I remembered the picture. The four of us, huddled together in the cold. A neighbour had taken it. We were standing outside a cottage we had rented when we lived in Whitby. David's hand touched my shoulder and I leant my head against it.

Suddenly I realised that I was kneeling on the grass outside the cottage. David and Mary had come with me.

'Portia, Susan!' mum yelled. 'Will you girls please stand still and smile for the camera?'

Her voice filled me with that sick feeling I had when I had been transported back in time before. I didn't want it to jolt me from the memory, so I took a deep breath and looked towards the scene before me.

'Right,' old Mr Glibb said, 'say cheese!' He had been our neighbour for years and loved to fuss around us, although he always pretended to have no time for children.

'Cheese,' we all chorused together as the camera snapped several times, the flash blinding the scene momentarily.

'Thank you, Mr Glibb,' I heard my dad say, walking forward to get his camera back. 'It's not often we get these two to stand still in one place, but we wanted a family photograph to send to my relatives in London.'

'London... a dreadful place,' Mr Glibb muttered.

'Couldn't agree more,' my mum said, giggling and walking forward to put her arms around my father's waist. 'I've been trying to persuade John that Whitby is the only place a person should be. He's been pestering me for years to make the move there.'

'I don't know about that,' Mr Glibb mused. 'I've heard of places with better weather, but I personally would never want to be anywhere else. It's a real place, Whitby; with real people. Not quite so soulless as the big city.'

'I'll bear that in mind,' my dad replied, smiling back.

Suddenly the sky seemed to darken and a rumble of thunder boomed overhead.

'Quick girls, get inside,' mum shouted, ushering the little version of myself back inside the house. I couldn't have been more than seven years old.

The happy little family that had once been mine hurried inside the house and closed the heavy wooden door behind them.

As the cottage door slammed shut another peal of thunder erupted around us and with a flash of lightning, the scene changed once more. I had expected us to be standing back in my bedroom, looking at the little photograph, but it seemed that my mind didn't want to let go of the happy memories just yet.

We were standing inside the cottage now, it was dark outside and the open fire crackled as bright orange flames licked their way towards the chimney.

I glanced around the vaguely familiar scene and saw that I was curled up on the sofa with my head in my mother's lap. She was stroking my hair and humming softly to herself.

'When's this one?' David asked in a whisper, not wanting to distract me in case we were taken from the memory.

'I'm not really sure, I wouldn't say it's a specific memory that I'm aware of; from the look of me I'm maybe about ten or eleven. It can't have been long before we ended up moving away.' I realised I was whispering too, even though I knew that there was no way anyone in the room could hear us. It was like the way you would speak to one another if you were watching a movie in the cinema.

As I said the words, the scene changed. I was hiding out on the dark stairs, watching my parents through a doorway into the living room. Mary, David and I were standing behind my childlike figure that was huddled on the staircase.

'It should have been a joint decision!' my mum bellowed.

'I have included you,' my dad pleaded.

'Really?' my mum asked sarcastically. 'I don't think this counts as including me John, you're not giving me a great deal of choice.'

'Look,' dad continued, 'I need to go where the work is, honey. You know I don't want to take you away from Whitby. We live on one income, I can't afford to turn down this opportunity.'

She looked hurt by his words. He knew it was a sore point for her that she didn't make much money running her pottery business. 'It's too much upset for the girls,' my mum said sulkily.

'They'll adjust,' my dad replied, sighing. 'Kids are resilient and London is a great place to be; great schools and lots of things to do at weekends. Plus, my parents would be really close by, that could be great.'

'So it's all about you going home to mummy then?' she asked bitterly.

'Of course not,' he said, sounding angrier than he had before. 'I didn't complain when you wanted to come back here. Coming back home…' he said in a mocking voice. 'You don't even have any family here, they're all dead!'

Silence; my mum hadn't responded to that.

'Jennifer, please,' my dad said, back to pleading once more.

A door opened and then slammed shut, out of sight at the back of the living room.

'Jennifer, where are you going!' my dad yelled; the door opening and closing once more.

The scene faded and now we were standing back in my bedroom, I would have had tears streaming down my face if I were capable of them.

'I know it's hard, but this is a good start, Portia,' Mary said, putting her hand on my shoulder.

'It's hard alright,' I whimpered, 'I don't know how it's helping, though.'

'You seem to be focussing on your mother,' Mary continued. 'Every memory you have relates to her, whether good or bad. Do you remember the day she left you?'

'Of course I do,' I said.

'Then perhaps that should be our next port of call,' Mary said, trying to reassure me. 'I think this will help you, Portia.'

I nodded without speaking and closed my eyes. After a few seconds I screwed up my face, desperately trying to focus my thoughts.

'Is something wrong?' David asked, his hand immediately reaching for my face in concern.

'I can't seem to remember it properly,' I muttered. 'I know what happened, but when I try to focus on the memory it seems fuzzy somehow.'

'Perhaps your mind has tried to block it out?' David asked, looking questioningly between Mary and myself.

'Perhaps,' Mary said, although she sounded as if she thought there might be another reason. 'Try to think of a time around then, did anything memorable happen?'

'I don't know,' I said, racking my brains to try to think of some memory that might help me trigger the one I needed to find. 'Susan's birthday,' I whispered.

'Your mother left soon after?' Mary asked.

'I think so,' I said, 'it was pretty bad. I'm sure she was gone within a few weeks of the party.'

'Let's do it,' David replied, taking my hand once more.

I closed my eyes and when I opened them again we were standing in the kitchen downstairs, with the mid afternoon sun streaming through the large window at the back of the room.

'Get the cake ready,' my mum said. She looked drained and unhappy. I turned to see who she was speaking to and saw my dad opening the fridge to remove a large chocolate cake and sit it on the counter where a bundle of candles sat ready to be placed on top.

At the opposite end of the room, Susan and I were sitting up at the scrubbed wooden kitchen table, with what looked like some of Susan's school friends gathered around us. It could have been mistaken for a rather jolly scene if the atmosphere between my parents hadn't been so icy. I didn't know whether all of the guests were aware of it, but it was obvious that Susan and I were. I must have been about seventeen, I didn't look as though I had changed.

My sister and I sat at the table with smiles on our faces, all the while casting sideways glances at our parents.

'Happy Birthday to you,' my dad started to sing as he walked forward with the cake. The teenagers around the table looked embarrassingly at one another for a few moments and then one by one joined in singing with him in a rather half-hearted manner.

My mum didn't join the chorus with the rest of us around the table. She poured a large glass of wine and walked into the living room.

The scene changed, it was later in the evening, but still the same day. I could see the balloons out in the hall. Once more, I was perched on a staircase, only this time, in our house in London. I might have been several years older, but sitting where I was, I looked just as scared and childlike as I had when I had huddled on the staircase in Whitby.

'Jennifer, what is wrong with you?' I heard my dad ask.

'I don't know what you mean,' my mum said, sounding disinterested.

'I knew you weren't happy about the move,' he continued, 'but I think you should let it go. It's been years now and the girls seemed to have settled in okay.'

'Believe me,' she said coldly, 'they haven't.'

I felt myself shiver. She was right. Susan was okay, she was always okay. I was miserable. I had never taken to life in London and I did my best to hide it from my dad. My mum on the other hand, made no effort to hide her feelings at all.

We flashed forward to another memory.

'Jennifer, don't do this!' my dad was shouting.

'I'm sorry, I can't stay here anymore,' she replied.

David, Mary and I were standing in my bedroom, while the live me was huddled on my bed listening to my parents arguing once more.

'Please,' dad begged, 'what do you want me to say?'

'There isn't anything to say,' mum quipped. 'You know how I feel, John. You know what this move has done to me. Why should we go over it again? You have your priorities and I have mine. If you really cared about us, you wouldn't have put me through this, have ignored the fact that I'm completely miserable here.'

'What about the girls?' he asked.

'Don't try the guilt trip, John,' she snapped back at him, opening their bedroom door and storming down the stairs. 'You think the girls are settled?' she bellowed. 'Give it a while, they'll walk out on you just like me!' The front door slammed.

'Well done,' Mary said, putting a hand on my shoulder. 'I know that can't have been easy.'

The memory shifted again and my dad was standing in the living room, shouting at my mum down the phone. 'Jennifer, don't you dare hang up on me.'

'I don't remember this,' I muttered. 'I can't see myself, how can I remember this?'

'Shh…' Mary said, 'just listen.'

'Where the hell is she?' my dad yelled.

'What do you mean who? Portia, your daughter, remember?' he continued.

'You're the one who gave her the idea,' he said, obviously hurt by some unheard jibe at the other end of the phone. 'She must have set off to find you. I know we don't have an address for you, but I'm sure she could figure it out.'

It was then that I saw myself in the scene, a very faint figure standing at the back of the room, almost unrecognisable.

'Dad,' my figure whispered. 'Dad, I'm here.'

'What the…' I panicked; my brain couldn't handle what was unfolding before me. The memory ended suddenly and we were all standing back in my darkened bedroom, the family picture in a frame standing before us. The warmth of that memory seemed a million miles away now.

'I was…' my voice trailed off.

'Dead?' Mary ventured.

'Yes,' I stuttered. 'I was dead in that scene, what does this mean. Can you travel to memories of your afterlife?'

'Yes,' Mary said, 'you just haven't had enough time among us to try.'

'Okay,' I muttered. 'I still don't remember actually dying. How can I have skipped the death part?'

'I'm not sure,' she replied. I know you don't have all the answers yet, but I think you understand things a little better.'

'How?' I asked. I was too freaked out to even be trying to think about things logically.

'Well,' David cut in, his voice startling me. 'I would guess that you ran away from home. From that conversation, at that point, neither of your parents knew that you had died. Your dad sounded really worried about you.'

I sat there for several moments letting what he had said sink in, trying to make it match up to the strange scene we had just plucked from my long lost memory. 'What now?' I asked eventually.

'That's up to you,' Mary said. 'Do you think you need to know more?'

'I don't know,' I replied, looking up at her. As soon as I looked into her face, I knew that wasn't true. I did need to know more. Where had I run off to? Was I killed in an accident?

'Yes,' Mary said nodding, it was as though she could read my mind, or my emotions anyway. 'Try and go back to that scene once more, it could trigger another memory for you.'

Once more we sat through that strange scene. Me a pale, ghostly spectre hovering in the background, while my dad phoned everyone he could think of trying to find me.

As my dad hung up the phone after what seemed like his hundredth call, the scene shifted. We were in the same place, but my dad was now sitting in his armchair, two police officers, a man and a woman, sitting across from him on the sofa.

I could see my dead self sitting at the kitchen table staring into space. It was as if I didn't actually see what was going on in the living room.

'I'm sorry, Mr Goldman,' the policewoman said.

'When did you find her?' dad asked.

'She washed up on shore this morning, some fishermen came across her body,' the policeman said, his eyes saddened by the news they had to deliver.

'When can I see her?' dad asked, his voice sounding strangely mechanical.

'We'll need you to come with us and make a formal identification,' the policeman continued. 'We're happy to arrange police transport to Whitby.'

'Thank you,' my dad replied. 'My daughter, Susan…' dad's voice trailed off.

'Do you have any family she could stay with?' the female officer asked.

'My parents could take her I suppose,' dad muttered.

'That's good, it's probably for the best,' the police woman said.

The scene faded once more. This time we were standing at a graveside. My dad and sister were standing together, both silently looking at the ground. At my dad's side, his parents stood, both looking sadly off into the distance.

There were few other people at the funeral, I noticed a couple of people I didn't recognise, probably colleagues of my dad and off in the distance a woman stood, trying her best to watch the ceremony without being seen.

It was next to her that I saw my ghostly self watching the scene with very little interest, almost as though I wasn't aware that it was going on.

The woman in the distance removed a pair of sunglasses from her face and dabbed her eyes with a handkerchief. It was my mother. I was standing right next to her and I hadn't realised.

In an instant David, Mary and I shifted and were standing next to my estranged mother. I just looked at her. She had known I was gone, had come to my funeral.

I looked around the place where was I buried; Prudence had made me wonder about that. I realised with a strange happiness that I was in Whitby. Dad had brought me home; I could smell the sea.

I saw the small group by the graveside break up and head back towards the cars which were assembled in the graveyard; no one noticed me or my mother standing in the background. I felt relief and wondered if that was coming from her.

'I think it's time to go home now,' David said, squeezing my hand.

I took one last look at my mother and nodded my head.

This time, rather than returning to my home, we actually re-materialised back in front of the manor.

'Do you need some time?' Mary asked.

'I...' I didn't really know what to say.

'I'll take care of her,' David said, taking me into his arms and fading from view.

'You're not going to leave again are you?' David asked me tentatively.

'No,' I muttered, opening my eyes to see where we were.

He had taken us to my room at the manor and laid me down upon the bed there.

'I wouldn't blame you,' he said, trying his best to sound supportive as he sat down gingerly at the end of the bed.

'I'm not going anywhere, David,' I said, sighing. 'Try not to panic.'

'You're telling me not to panic?' he asked, looking at me strangely. 'I thought you would be *freaking out*, as you put it.'

I laughed weakly. 'Who says I'm not.'

He crawled warily up the bed towards me and lay down beside me, never taking his eyes from my face the entire time.

'Honestly,' I said, trying to reassure him. 'I'm not going to run off. I am freaked out, but in some ways, this is a good thing. At least I know what happened, kind of.

At least I know that my family did care about me, that my mum…' I trailed off.

'She did love you, Portia,' he said, stroking my face. 'You could tell. She was just a very unhappy woman.'

'Yes,' I muttered, feeling that I should be crying.

David could sense my distress and he took me into his arms, with his chin resting upon the top of my head. It was strange, he seemed to be able to sense my emotions just as easily as Mary could. I wondered whether he had some kind of gift, or whether it was something that came from the bond between us. I thought I could read him pretty well, but it wasn't the same. He could read me like a book.

'I think Mary was right, this is probably better for you. You know the truth now, it could help you to make peace with the existence we have here.'

'Yes,' I muttered. It had achieved that in one sense. Since I had found out the truth, I hadn't been considering trying to find a way into heaven. In fact, subconsciously, I think I was focussed upon something else. I wanted to find my mother.

I think he could sense that too. 'Where do we start?' he asked.

I smiled at him weakly. How could I have ever contemplated leaving him? I had never known anyone who understood me so well. I reached up and kissed him, a non existent tear brushing my cheek.

He pulled away and looked at me, confused. 'Is everything okay?' he asked, concerned by my sudden rush of emotion.

'Everything's fine,' I said, reassuringly. 'There's only one place *to* start.'

'Where?' David asked.

'As Prudence says,' I replied, 'all roads lead to Whitby.'

Chapter Thirteen
A Place By The Sea

David wasted no time, he took my hand and before I knew it, we were standing in the graveyard by the sea. I was grateful he was so eager to see this through with me, whatever it might mean. It wasn't going to be easy, but hopefully it would help me lay my demons to rest, well, at least some of them.

'So what now?' he asked, looking around the place. It was dusk and the graveyard did look decidedly creepy.

'It's getting dark,' I replied. 'Perhaps we should visit Prudence and her friends; they might be able to offer some advice.'

'Sure,' he said, striding forward towards the crypt, all social awkwardness he had felt upon our last visit here, completely gone. I think our love had filled him with a new-found confidence in himself. I knew he had given me more confidence. This type of love made me feel more grounded, more tangible somehow.

I hesitated for a moment, unsure whether it was rude to enter their home without permission, even though I knew my previous visit would mean I was guaranteed entry.

'Come in,' Prudence's sharp voice echoed from inside. I smiled. She was obviously doing her best to sound grumpy. If she knew it was me, it must have been an act. She did like to appear stern, even through her eyes never failed to give her away.

We materialised inside the crypt to find Prudence and Jonah sitting upon their usual tomb, they were playing cards.

'Where did you find those?' I asked, looking at the deck strewn in front of them.

'Well, what an impertinent question!' she exclaimed, glancing round at me. 'Did your parents never teach you the normal salutations? How about: Hello, dear Prudence, how the devil are you?'

'I'm sorry,' I replied, grinning, 'Hello, Prudence. I hope you're well.'

'Much better,' she said, rising from her seat and carefully sitting her cards down to ensure that Jonah wouldn't see her hand. 'I am well thank you, my dear. To what do we owe this pleasure?'

'It's so good to see you,' Jonah piped up.

Prudence shot him a glance as though she was not happy at being interrupted.

'It's good to see you too, Jonah,' I said, smiling at the old gentleman, his phantom pipe still protruding from his mouth. 'We're here for your help.'

'I'm intrigued,' Prudence said, a flicker of a smile on her lips, 'do, tell.'

'I need to find my mother, and I believe she's here in Whitby,' I continued, spluttering out my request, somehow nervous.

'Obviously a woman of taste,' Prudence said, 'the best people live here.'

Jonah chuckled.

'Is she one of us? That might make it easier; we have quite a wide network of the dead in this town, you know. Very well connected, I have friends from every generation.'

'Thank you,' I said, feeling that she had misunderstood. 'Unfortunately, she isn't one of us.'

'Really?' Prudence mused. 'In that case, what's the point?'

'Well…' I said, feeling rather sheepish.

'She doesn't want to talk to her,' David cut in, suspecting I needed some help. 'She merely wishes to know where she is, that she's alright. They lost touch before Portia passed away.'

'A shame,' Jonah mused, 'but it happens so often; a family feud?'

'Of sorts,' I replied, uncomfortably.

'Portia's mother had a disagreement with her father; it meant that all contact was severed,' David qualified.

I was glad he had spoken; I wasn't sure whether I wanted to go into such detail.

'I see,' Prudence's face was full of compassion. 'It's always hardest on the children. Not something that happened in my day, but this younger generation seems to have no sense of right and wrong.'

'Don't kid yourself,' Jonah snorted. 'Just wasn't talked about is all. I knew plenty of families where the man had either gone off to sea and settled with a wench elsewhere, or simply never been heard of again.'

Prudence shook her head. 'Nonsense,' she muttered. 'Anyway, where to start…'

'Did you have other family from the town, family that's deceased I mean,' Jonah said, an idea obviously brewing.

'My mum's family belonged here for generations, although they died when she was rather young,' I told him, curious as to what he was considering.

'Could be,' he mused, 'we may know of your grandparents, or some such further back. What was her name?'

'She was called Jennifer Goldman,' I said without thinking.

'I don't know of any Goldman's around here,' Jonah said, disappointed.

'Wait,' I said suddenly, 'that was her married name. Her maiden name was Harland. She was called, Jennifer Harland.'

'Ah,' Jonah said, smiling, Prudence also desperate to chime in. 'We know of some Harlands,' he said.

Prudence nodded. 'That we do. There is a charming lady who resides locally by the name of Hortense Harland. I dare say her mother had airs about her, hence the silly name.'

'Hortense,' I mused, 'I think that might be my great grandmother or my great, great grandmother. I definitely know the name.'

'Well, it's not a bad place to start then, is it,' Prudence said, smiling. 'Let's go.'

She stood up and, taking Jonah's hand, she stretched the other out for me to hold.

'Now?' I asked, slightly taken aback at the thought of meeting one of my ancestors.

'What are we waiting for?' she asked.

I looked over at David, feeling startled. He shrugged his shoulders, so I took a deep breath, grabbed his hand and reached out for Prudence with the other.

'Here we go,' Jonah said, smiling as the crypt dissipated into nothing.

As my eyes adjusted I could see that we were standing in an old shop. The whole place was boarded up and closed and it felt as though no-one had occupied the space for quite some time. There were musty boxes piled up on the floor and the bay window, once used for display had been boarded up.

'Service!' Prudence called, her voice raised jovially, pretending to ring a bell on the counter in front of her.

'Really, Prudence,' a lady said, bustling out from the back of the shop. I don't know what I had expected, but it wasn't this lady. She must have been of a similar age to

Prudence, but she was wearing a rather outlandish bright pink frock that seemed to clash with Prudence's austere black attire, even though it was shrouded with our deathly grey hue. She had large bosoms, something which I definitely hadn't inherited, and even in death, she obviously liked showing them off.

'You will keep this up,' she bustled, ready to chastise her latest customer. 'You know I'm not open for business... Oh...' She was taken aback when she saw that her friend had brought company. 'It's always a pleasure, Jonah,' she said, nodding to Prudence's companion. 'Who are these... other people?'

'These, are my friends, Portia and David,' Prudence said, motioning to us in turn. 'They are on a mercy mission and I was hoping you might be able to help.'

'Right,' Hortense said, looking at us, confused. 'I'm not sure what help I can be, my dear. I only reside here in my shop. It's not what it used to be, but it's still home. The last lot who rented tried to make it into some kind of ghastly herbal remedies store. I ask you! In my day, it was the best tearoom on Church Street. Everyone came to taste my scones.'

'You deviate from the point a little, dear,' Prudence said, smiling kindly, 'but thank you for the trip down memory lane. We believe this young lady is a relative of yours.'

'Really?' Hortense said, screwing her eyes up as she considered me, as though this would somehow help her recognise me. 'She looks a bit of a puny thing. We Harlands were usually built to last.'

'Did you have any knowledge of her mother?' Prudence continued, ignoring her friend's insult. 'She's a Jennifer Harland, still living.'

'I'm not sure,' Hortense said, again screwing up her eyes and trying to think.

'Forgive her,' Prudence whispered in an aside to me. 'It happens when we choose to live in solitude. Sometimes the mind fills with cobwebs.'

'Ahem,' Hortense said, trying to draw attention back to herself, something which she obviously enjoyed. It seemed strange to me that someone who was used to commanding attention would chose to live in alone.

'I think she might have been your granddaughter, or great granddaughter, I can't be sure,' I said, trying to help her along. 'I can't remember my grandmother's name, I only remembered yours because it was so unusual.'

'Why, thank you, my dear,' the old lady replied, smiling with pride.

'Hortense, please,' Prudence said, trying to focus her friend once more.

Eventually, Hortense seemed to remember something. 'It was a long time ago, but I remember that my grandson Robert had a baby called Jennifer. Back then, I used to check in on the living family, you know how it is, but you lose track. They lived in a cottage up on Henrietta Street.'

'A good place to start,' Prudence said, glancing at me.

'I don't know,' I said doubtfully. 'If mum was ever there, how likely is it she would be there now. We didn't live there when I was young.'

'You never know,' Jonah said, trying to remain hopeful. 'Maybe we'll find another clue there? Or someone else like us who may be able to help. Lots of us return to where we lived.'

'Why do you live in a graveyard then?' David asked. I could tell that the question had slipped out without his meaning it to.

Prudence looked irritated, 'Because the ghastly younger generation pulled our houses down!'

'Not quite in my case,' Jonah said, trying to lighten the situation. 'Mine fell into the sea.'

David and I giggled.

Prudence huffed. 'Must we really waste time on these ridiculous meanderings? Hmm?'

'Of course,' I said. 'Sorry, Prudence.'

'Right,' she replied. 'Thank you, Hortense, you have been most helpful.'

'Stop by again soon,' she said, smiling, yet slightly bewildered. She then turned and disappeared back into the darkness of the shop.

We were standing outside.

'Is she alright?' I asked. 'I would have thought she would be a little bit more interested in me.'

'She's a well-meaning woman, but her brain's a bit addled,' Prudence explained. 'As I said, too much time alone.'

'Your brain's already addled,' David said to me with a smirk. 'We'll need to watch these sulking sessions of yours; if it runs in the family, you'll end up barmy.'

I elbowed him in the ribs, but couldn't help laughing.

'David, really,' Prudence said, but I could tell she wanted to laugh just as much as I did. I heard Jonah let out a raspy chuckle behind me.

'Onwards, people!' Prudence said in a commanding voice, holding her hands out once more. She was like a strange-looking tour guide or a military sergeant. We were just her troops, dawdling behind her.

'So we're going to Henrietta Street?' I asked, feeling as if this was a bit of a long shot.

'Better than nothing,' Prudence said. 'I'm not usually one for snooping...'

Jonah choked for a moment and Prudence shot him an icy glance.

'However,' she continued,' I think if we pop our heads into a few of the cottages up there, we're sure to find something.'

'Let's go,' David said, taking hold of my hand. 'It's better than nothing, and besides, this is actually fun. I'm beginning to understand the inner workings of your mind a little better. Maybe the next ancestor of yours we bump into will have no sense of direction, just like you.' He grinned.

Considering that this had started off as a rather serious personal journey for me, it seemed to be descending into a complete farce, and David looked as though he was having the time of his life. I sighed and took his hand. If nothing came of this, at least it was an adventure. I could picture Beth laughing aloud when we described Hortense to her.

Henrietta Street was a rather quaint little road lined with terraced houses and at the end of it, you could see the sea. I wasn't sure where exactly would be the best place to start.

David could sense my unease. 'Let's just start at the beginning,' he said, motioning for us to enter the first house on the left.

We hesitated on the threshold, feeling rather unsure, and then went to enter the doorway. It seemed to be blocked.

'What does this mean?' I asked, looking at Prudence.

'It means, that one of our kind resides here, and as such, it's protected. I'm sure we'll be able to attract their attention. It looks a nice, rather well-tended sort of place, I wouldn't think it will be someone unseemly.'

'Okay,' I said, waiting for her to work her magic.

She cleared her throat, 'Hello,' she chirruped, almost singing the word.

'What do you want?' a grumpy voice asked.

I leapt back off the doorstep as an old man's head appeared through the door itself, grimacing at us. For a second, I thought it was Mr Weatherby, but I realised it was just someone of a similar disposition.

'We are looking for a family by the name of Harland,' Prudence said, trying to keep her composure, despite her obvious disgust at the man's lack of manners. 'Do you know which house they resided in?' She sounded incredibly formal as she spoke, yet her face revealed exactly what she thought of this gentleman.

'Hmm,' the man said, eying us suspiciously. 'I think they lived at number eight, but that was a long time ago; I don't know that you'll find them there now.'

'Thank you,' Prudence said, nodding to the man.

Jonah went to doff his cap and David and I simply shuffled away as quickly as we could. I didn't dare look round, but I could tell that he watched our progress as we walked up the street.

'Ghastly,' Prudence muttered once we were out of earshot.

'Don't judge, Prudence,' Jonah said, taking her hand. 'Maybe he doesn't have the love of a good woman.'

'Really!' Prudence blushed.

I hadn't thought about it before, but they were an odd couple. Prudence was so hopelessly formal and uptight, whereas Jonah was a down to earth, working-class man. He definitely didn't seem the kind of gentleman that it would have been acceptable for Prudence to be associated with in her living life. The way she spoke sometimes, I got the impression that she had been a spinster when alive. It was nice to think she had found love in this life. Somehow, they worked. I dare say David and I didn't look as though we belonged together either.

When we arrived at the house, we all hesitated. It looked as though it was lived in. The light around us had started to fade, and there were lamps lit inside the place.

'Should we try walking in?' Jonah asked, trying to peer through the window.

'Why not,' I said, taking the lead. I don't know where my bravado was coming from. Maybe it was because Prudence and Jonah had somehow made this whole thing seem light-hearted.

I stepped in the door and the others followed me. There obviously weren't other dead people in the place, which somehow made my heart sink. If there was only a living family in the house, we wouldn't be able to get any more information.

'Don't lose heart,' David said, taking my hand. 'Let's have a look around first.'

I smiled, my bravery wavering slightly as we both walked into the front room.

If I had been alive, my heart would have stopped. There, sitting on an armchair by the fire, was my mother. She was sitting peacefully reading a book. She looked serene and the light of the flames bounced off the blonde hair that tumbled down her shoulders.

As we all entered, I noticed that she shivered a little, lifted a blanket from the back of the chair and placed it over her legs.

'This is her?' Prudence asked, whispering, despite the fact there was no way my mother could hear her.

'Yes,' I answered in hushed tones, 'it's her.'

'I can see the resemblance,' Prudence said, considering the living woman before us.

'She looks okay,' David said, trying to reassure me.

'I can't believe she's here,' I muttered.

'Was she close to her own mother?' Prudence asked. 'Perhaps she wanted to be back in the last place she remembered her.

'Perhaps,' I said, unable to take my eyes off the all too familiar woman in front of me. 'Her mother died when she was young. She never spoke about her much, but I know it was because of her that we lived in Whitby. I think she always felt the need to be close to her.'

The strangest feeling washed over me as I looked at her. It didn't make sense to me, but somehow I felt bitter. I had wanted to see her, see that she was okay, but at the same time I resented her. She was sitting in her cosy little house, looking utterly content, when she had been the one who had walked out on all of us. Her decision had cost me my life, yet she seemed completely at ease.

I don't know what came over me, but I couldn't help myself. I walked towards her, knelt down in front of her and looked up into her face. 'Why?' I muttered. I didn't know what else to say, I just didn't understand. Even if she had been unhappy, it didn't make any sense that she didn't want to take Susan and I with her. I would still have been alive if she had. At least, I might have been.

As I spoke, she looked up from her book. For a terrified moment, I thought she had heard me, that she was going to answer me.

She didn't say anything. After a fleeting glance in my direction, she turned and gazed into the flames. Staring blankly, her book slid from her grasp and flopped onto the floor; she began to cry. 'I'm sorry,' she muttered, her dazzling blue eyes awash with tears.

'Did she hear me?' I asked, feeling a mixture of fear and excitement. Had I reached her?

'I don't think she heard your words, dear,' Jonah said, moving towards me. 'I think she felt you though. At least you know she misses you; that she thinks of you.'

'Yes,' I muttered, still staring at her beautiful face. 'I guess so. Why doesn't that make me feel any better?'

'It should,' David said, kneeling down next to me and putting an arm around my shoulders. 'Now you have one more place to visit. You can check in on her, keep her in your life.'

'One more place to run off to,' I said, smiling sadly. 'I wouldn't have thought that would appeal to you.'

'I don't mind where you run,' he said, stroking my hair, 'as long as you always come home.'

'Home,' I muttered. 'I can't judge her, I'm no different. I ran away from my living family and it cost me my life. Now I keep running away from you. The irony is that she has run back to a place which is filled with nothing but ghosts for her. I wish I could tell her that she has a choice. That she could still be with her family if she wanted to. She may have lost me, but she still has one daughter who needs her.'

'She'll need to figure that out for herself,' Prudence said knowingly. 'The same way you did. And, she will. Whether it will be too late or not is down to her, but it's not your job to fix this. Everyone has to find their own path. Unfortunately, the benefit of hindsight we have, cannot be passed on to those we leave behind.'

'I know,' I said, standing up. 'Thank you,' I continued, turning to face Prudence and Jonah. Moments earlier, I had thought I might cry, but that seemed to have passed. I felt grateful to my friends. 'You've really helped me today. I don't know how to repay you.'

'Don't mention it, my dear,' Prudence said, reaching out for my hand. 'Are you ready to leave?'

I walked forward to take it. 'Yes,' I said, and as the room faded, I had one last glance back at my mother's face. I didn't want to leave her, but I was sure of one thing, this wasn't my home. Not any more.

We arrived back in the crypt and Jonah settled himself down in his usual seat again. 'Well that was a little adventure, we don't have those every day.'

'Indeed,' Prudence said, picking up her hand of cards. 'You run along back to where you belong,' she said, her voice stern once more, but I knew she was joking.

'I will,' I said, squeezing David's hand. 'Thank you, again.'

'Not at all,' Prudence said once more. 'Just make sure you visit.'

'Definitely,' I said, smiling.

'Either that, or drag this one to that grand house of yours so she can hear the piano,' Jonah said, winking.

Prudence looked a bit taken aback, but didn't say anything.

'We will,' I said. 'I promise. One more thing…'

'Yes?' Prudence asked, sighing.

'You never did tell me where you got those playing cards?' I asked, grinning.

Prudence tutted. 'You are nosy aren't you.'

I laughed. 'Well?'

'Someone dropped them in the graveyard,' Jonah said. 'They're a bit musty, but that doesn't bother us; helps to pass the time.'

'Right,' I said. 'Well have fun!'

'We will,' Prudence said, fighting a smile. 'Now, shoo!'

With that, David and I faded from the crypt and rematerialised back in my bedroom at the manor.

'Are you going to be okay?' he asked.

'I think I will,' I said, smiling.

'And just where have you two been?' Mary asked, appearing in my doorway, Beth sheepishly hovering behind her.

'We went on a little adventure,' David said.

'One I would approve of?' Mary asked.

'We went back to Whitby,' I said, trying to calm her worries. 'I wanted to find my mother.'

'Oh,' Mary said, taken aback. I could tell she was curious at this turn of events. 'And were you successful?'

'Yes,' I said, 'I think we were. I know where I belong now.'

'Good,' she said, beaming.

At this, Beth ran past her and jumped onto my bed. 'Tell me all about it. I can't believe I missed another trip to the seaside.'

David and I laughed.

'It's funny,' he said, 'we've been trying to talk Portia's friend, Prudence into making a trip here. Maybe you two would get along.'

We then told Beth all the details and she laughed and gasped her way through the story. She loved hearing of such adventures, but I still wasn't convinced she would want to go on one herself. What did that matter? When we were here together, the whole world didn't matter.

Chapter Fourteen
Sunny Days And Sandy Beaches

The time that passed after that day was perhaps the happiest of my life, of either of my lives. David and I were blissfully content and it felt as if I might finally have left my troubles behind me.

The fact that I knew my living family had moved on with their lives, meant I didn't have to visit them so much, I knew they were happy, or I hoped they were at least.

As ever, time seemed to keep shifting, and I now didn't have any proper frame of reference for how long had passed since my adventure had begun. It stopped being important when you were as content as this. I was sure that Mary didn't wholeheartedly approve, but that didn't seem to matter either. I didn't think anything would be able to burst my bubble.

David, Beth and I had a great deal of fun together, and David's and my relationship went from strength to strength. I think he believed me now; I wasn't going to run away again, I was happy, exactly where I was. When I thought of my strange longing for the other side, it seemed a lifetime ago. For a while after things had settled down, I had noticed him watching me from time to time. It happened when we were apart, or at least, at a distance from one another. He would watch me, his eyes cautious. It was as though he was trying to figure out what I was thinking; paranoid that my thoughts might be drifting back to a darker place.

I managed to win his trust eventually, I think. He realised that he couldn't watch me all the time, and just because I wasn't at his side, it didn't mean I was going to disappear either.

Beth's confidence seemed to be increasing too. She now allowed us to sit and listen to her play piano in the music room, although David and I were the only permitted audience. I know that Mary would have loved to join us, but it actually felt quite nice when it was just the three of us. It was like being part of an exclusive club. We seemed to strike a comfortable balance together and despite her misgivings, Mary couldn't help but notice how we were all blossoming.

We visited Whitby as often as we could, and I tried my hardest to convince Prudence that she should come with us to visit the manor. We tried the same approach to get Beth to go to the seaside, but neither of them had been convinced to leave their respective homes as yet. I wouldn't let it go, I knew they would love a change of scenery and for Beth, I hoped it might help build her confidence even more. It was obvious that she was sad any time David and I left her; a little of the light around her seemed to fade. I don't know whether it was our company she was sad to lose, or whether a little part of her was disappointed in herself. Where we went, she couldn't follow. I hoped it was the latter, because at least then, David and I would be able to help her. We wouldn't have to feel so guilty at leaving her when we had to.

She was sitting looking forlorn on the bottom step in the hall as David and I tried, once more, to convince her she should come with us.

'You might enjoy yourself,' I said, smiling at her pleadingly.

'I don't know, Portia,' she replied, looking terrified at the prospect.

'I'll be right there,' David said, reaching out for her hand, 'and if you feel at all uncomfortable, I can always bring you home. But I think Portia's right. It's time you expanded your horizons. Who knows what new things could come into your life if you venture out of doors?'

She shied away from his hand as though it might hurt her, and looked at me with confused eyes.

'We're not going to force you,' I said reassuringly. The last thing I wanted to do was to frighten her. She had come so far, we didn't want to damage that.

'Are you sure I'd be safe?' she asked. 'There are bad people, like that man who found Portia before.'

'You'll be perfectly safe with me,' David said, smiling at his sister patiently. 'Besides, that man latched onto Portia because she's an idiot.'

I glowered at him.

He smiled and continued, 'what I meant to say was, she didn't know what she was doing and she didn't have protection. You do, you have me.'

Slowly, she held out her hand and took hold of David's. Her little hand looked so delicate in his. I could see Mary standing at the other end of the hall smiling. She had never known how to bring Beth out of herself fully and I think she was delighted at the thought of the young girl venturing beyond the boundaries of the manor.

I grinned to myself. Perhaps now, I had ceased to be a project for her, no longer the problem child.

We materialised in the graveyard and Beth looked completely petrified.

'Where is this?' she asked, her eyes like saucers. 'Where have you taken me?'

'It's just the graveyard,' I said, squeezing her hand. 'Remember, this is where we said we met Prudence and Jonah. We've told you about it dozens of times, there's nothing to be afraid of here.'

'Ah,' she said, her breathing slowing a little, but not much.

'That's the sea, out there,' I said pointing toward the cliffs, 'we'll see more of it when we head to the beach. That little building over there is the crypt where Prudence and Jonah live with their friends. It sounds kind of creepy, but they actually make it feel like home.'

'It's so strange,' she said, peering across the graveyard at the marble tomb.

'Would you like to meet them?' I asked. 'I've told them all about you. They're really nice people, I'm sure you would hit if off right away.'

'Really?' she asked, embarrassed at the thought of a stranger knowing anything about her. Sometimes I forgot how shy she was; it was easily done when you knew her so well.

'Yes,' I said, starting to walk towards the crypt. 'Prudence is a lovely woman, and I think the two of you will get along really well.'

David disappeared from my side and re-materialised leaning nonchalantly against the wall of the crypt. I didn't know whether he was trying to appear confident to inspire Beth, or if he was just showing off. A part of me hoped that Prudence would stick her head through the door and tell him off for leaning on someone's tomb, but I suppose that would be unseemly behaviour for a lady.

'Come along,' I coaxed, pausing for a moment while Beth was still rooted to the spot.

'Okay,' she said, hurrying to catch up with me. Obviously the thought of being left behind was worse than the prospect of meeting strangers for the first time. I made a mental note to remember that; it could be useful in the future. I wanted to be as kind as possible, but at the same time, it was obvious that she needed a little push.

As we approached the building where my friends lived, Prudence materialised outside. We had grown close over the last few months and she now knew my presence well enough to realise when I was close by.

'Hello, my dear,' she said, smiling broadly. 'David, it's always a pleasure,' she continued, tutting as she noticed his stance.

I smiled.

David nodded to her, standing up straight.

'And who might this be?' she asked, looking at Beth, who had moved and was doing her best to hide behind her brother. 'Have you brought along a new little stray?'

'No,' I replied, smiling. 'This is, Beth,' I motioned for her to step forward. 'She's David's sister. We've told you about her before.'

'Of course,' Prudence said, smiling, 'the piano virtuoso.'

'Oh,' Beth said, even more embarrassed than she had been before. 'I don't know about that,' she stuttered. 'I do enjoy playing, but I'm not very good.'

'I would love to hear you sometime,' Prudence said, smiling.

'That is an honour reserved for very few people,' David joked, 'although I'm sure the two of you will be fine friends in no time. You both have a dislike of leaving the places where you live.'

'Indeed,' Prudence said, keeping her distance from the young girl in case she might frighten her off. 'Why are you scallywags here today then?' she asked. 'Not that I'm not always delighted to see you.'

'We're taking Beth to the beach,' I said, grinning. 'The sun was shining, so we thought we would make the most of it.'

'Capital idea,' Prudence replied. 'Perhaps Jonah and I could join you? We've been spending a little bit too much time indoors these days, and you know how detrimental that can be.'

'Yes,' I said, nodding, my mind drifting to my long dead, yet slightly barmy relative. 'Have you spoken with Hortense lately? I do worry about her sometimes. She is family after all.'

'I check in on her when I can,' Prudence said, shaking her head. 'It's impossible to get the woman to go out. I've tried telling her that she would be welcome staying with us, but she refuses to leave her shop behind. Some people do have an irrational attachment to the past.'

Beth shuffled, looking sheepish. Obviously Prudence's words were making her feel uncomfortable.

David smiled at her. 'Don't worry, Beth, you have a long way to go before you end up like Hortense Harland. Trust me…'

Beth smiled.

'I'll be right back,' Prudence said, vanishing once more.

In no time at all, she re-materialised with Jonah standing beside her. I couldn't help but burst out laughing when I saw him. He still had his flat cap on his head, and his pipe in his mouth, but he appeared to be wearing some kind of faded Victorian swim suit.

'Jonah, honestly,' Prudence said, shaking her head.

'What?' he asked, grinning from ear to ear. 'I thought we were going to the beach?'

'Are you planning on swimming?' I asked. It was something I had tried myself on one of our visits, but it was rather difficult to control your movements in the water when it kept on passing through you. Rather than moving through the water, you simply moved with it. It was incredibly disorientating.

'I might dip a toe in the water,' he said, putting his hands on his hips. 'I was a champion swimmer in my day.'

'I think the point is,' Prudence said, amusement creeping into her tone, despite the fact she was trying to sound serious, 'that your day was not yesterday.'

'I like it,' I said, smiling at him.

'Thank you,' Jonah replied, making a mock bow. 'Shall we?'

'Let's' Prudence said, vanishing on the spot. As she faded, she was shaking her head and looking at Jonah.

David took Beth's hand and the three of us also vanished and re-appeared on the beach. Prudence had already selected a spot and was sitting looking out to sea, Jonah sitting happily at her side.

I studied Beth for a moment, eager to see her reaction to the place.

'This is wonderful,' Beth said eventually, evidently feeling happy for the first time since we had left the house. 'I wish I could feel the sea breeze on my face. I always wanted to go to the seaside when I was alive.'

'I know,' I replied, frustrated, 'but it's still fun here. Take a leaf from Jonah's book. He's determined to get into the spirit of things, even if he can't actually go swimming.'

We spent the next few hours laughing and frolicking on the sand. It was still early spring, so there weren't a great deal of tourists in the town yet. The beach was never as much fun when it was crowded with living people. They got in the way.

I had completely lost track of time, delighted at the fun that Beth was having running along the beach, when something suddenly stabbed into my senses.

It was an odd feeling, something almost familiar, but also terrifying. I turned around, and to my horror I saw a lone figure standing upon the cliffs looking down. I don't know how I knew, but even at this distance, I knew who it was.

Before I even thought about it, I was suddenly standing up on the cliff top beside her. Susan, was standing looking out to sea, her face, wet with tears.

'What are you doing here?' I asked instinctively. It was frustrating that I didn't get an answer.

'Why…' she muttered. Her hurt reached out and seemed to pull the heart from my chest. I wondered if she was here because of mum, or because of me. I had asked the same question when I had seen her. Although I was all too aware that my own passing must have caused her the same amount of hurt and confusion.

Staring around the place, I couldn't see anyone else. My mum definitely wasn't there; I'd have been able to sense her.

Something was wrong; I could feel it in the pit of my stomach. Whatever she was doing here, it wasn't sightseeing. I could feel panic coursing through me, not aided by the fact that I felt completely helpless.

David appeared next to me. 'What's wrong?' he asked, looking around him, expecting there to be some kind of threat.

'It's Susan,' I said, motioning to her. 'I don't know what she's doing here, but something isn't right.'

'What should we do?' he asked.

'I don't know,' I said. 'You stay with Beth, she couldn't cope with jumping around all over the place and I need to check in on my dad.'

'Okay,' he said warily. I knew he didn't want me going off on my own, but he couldn't argue with me. Going off and leaving Beth just now would be the worst thing he could do; she would never leave the house again.

I kissed him softly. 'I love you,' I said, as my body faded from view.

'I love you too...' I heard as his voice drifted away.

When I arrived at my dad's house, the place was in complete uproar.

'Where is she?' my dad was yelling, completely panic stricken. My grandmother was sitting opposite him.

'Stay calm, dear,' she said, trying desperately to comfort him.

'Calm?' he spat. 'How can I stay calm, mum? I've already lost one daughter. I can't lose another.'

'You're not going to lose her,' gran said, moving over and putting an arm around him. 'Just think calmly, where would she go?'

'I don't know!' he cried, his head in his hands. 'I've tried all her friends, but I did that last time. I can't believe this is happening again. Things seemed to be getting better, I thought we were moving forward.'

'What about Jennifer?' she asked. The way she said my mother's name held a hint of disgust.

'I don't really know where she is,' he said, shrugging his shoulders. 'I think she's in Whitby, but I don't have an address or a telephone number. Don't you think if I did, I would have been on the phone? After what happened with Portia, she changed her mobile number.'

I felt frantic, the emotions pouring from my father seeping into me. 'Dad!' I shouted. 'She's in Whitby, you have to go to Whitby!'

He looked up towards me and for a moment, it seemed as though he was looking right at me. Then he stood up from his chair and muttered, 'Whitby...'

'You think she could be there?' my grandmother asked.

'I don't know,' he said, looking confused. 'Something's telling me to go there, and it's where Portia went after all. Maybe Susan's gone looking for her mother as well.'

'Okay,' my grandmother replied. 'I'll stay here. We'll need to have someone at the house in case she comes back. Be careful, and let me know when you get there.'

'I will,' he said, grabbing his car keys and coat and running for the door.

'Drive carefully!' she shouted as the door slammed behind him.

Frustrated, I took one last look around the room and then I was back on the cliff top next to Susan. It was going to take dad hours to get to Whitby and Susan looked completely distraught; so much so, she looked as though she might do something stupid.

'Susan,' I said, desperately trying to reach her. It seemed to have worked with dad. 'Step away from the edge, it's not safe here.'

She glanced around at me, but didn't move an inch. 'Portia...' she said, staring blindly across the water. 'Is it better to be free of all this? Did you want to leave us?'

'No,' I said, reaching out and touching her hand. 'I didn't mean to leave you, at least, I don't think I did.'

As my hand touched hers she gasped. I hoped this might convince her to step away from the edge, but to my horror, she seemed to slip and lose her balance. Fighting with every ounce of strength I possessed, I tried to reach out and grab hold of her, but her body went right through my fingers and she plummeted towards the water below.

'No!' I screamed, appearing back on the beach and staring out at the water. After a few moments, desperately scanning the thrashing grey sea, I could see her body. She looked as though she was struggling to keep her head above the water.

'Swim, Susan, swim!' I yelled out to her. I had never felt so completely helpless.

David and Beth were at the other end of the beach, I knew David could sense my upset, but he was obviously trying to guard Beth from what was going on.

My body convulsed as a man ran through me and out into the water.

For the first time, I didn't care about the nauseous feeling caused by human contact. He was wading out into the water to help Susan and that was all that mattered. After a few minutes, which seemed like hours, he struggled back to the shore holding her limp body in his arms. I stood, unmoving, not daring to breathe as he lay her down on the sand and opened her mouth.

'No,' I muttered, looking at her blue skin and purple lips. 'Please, no...'

'Portia?' I didn't want to turn around, but I knew I had no choice. Slowly, I turned my head and there she was, standing beside me. 'Portia, what is this?' she asked.

'Susan,' I cried, 'oh, Susan, what have you done?'

'I didn't mean to,' she said, still confused.

Just then it happened. I was so close to it, the overwhelming feeling seemed to crush me. It was the light. The light had come for Susan, of course it would. She was still a child after all, at least technically.

'No!' I heard David yell, but it was too late.

I didn't walk into the light, it took me. It had come for my sister, but I was so close to her, that it simply swallowed me whole. I tried to yell to David, tried to reach out, but there was nothing I could do. I wasn't leaving him, I was being taken.

Before I knew it, there was no beach, no sea, no David, not even any Susan. That didn't make sense to me. I lifted my hand to my eyes to shield myself from the light which completely surrounded me. The only thing that I could feel was warmth. It wasn't the same as the sensation I felt with David; it was gentle, but at the same time, it was more permanent. It radiated from every inch of my body.

'Portia?' a strange voice said in the distance.

'Hello,' I said, my voice echoing in the bright empty space.

'We need to talk,' the unknown voice said, taking my hand.

My eyes were still completely blinded, but I took the stranger's hand and willingly followed them, walking forward. Despite my confusion, I had never felt so at peace; so completely content.

'Where is this?' I asked, realising that my voice seemed to echo in the cavernous space.

'It's the waiting room, of course,' the voice said. 'Come, take a seat.'

I sat down on a highly polished chair and my eyes seemed to adjust to my surroundings.

'Oh, my,' I said, completely lost for words.

Chapter Fifteen
The Interview

I sat staring at the room around me. It was surreal. I wasn't the only one sitting in the large waiting room and this made the whole situation seem even stranger. The entire room was bathed with light, but now that I could focus, I noticed that I appeared to be in a plush office of some kind. Obviously we had left behind the cavernous room I had arrived in, and now there were white leather sofas lining the walls, with several doorways spaced in between.

The white doors had frosted glass along the top half and each one seemed to have gold writing embossed upon it. Screwing up my eyes, I tried to make out what was written on the one closest to me. It wasn't particularly easy to read in the brightness and I was frightened to get up from my seat, in case that would be breaking some unwritten rule.

'Interview Room One…' I muttered to myself as I finally managed to read it. *That doesn't sound good*, I thought. Despite my cheerfully bright surroundings, the title made me think of a police station; a place for wrongdoers like me.

I then tried to glance discreetly at the people sitting around me. They were a very odd bunch. I would say that most of them looked to be from my own time, but there were a few who looked as though they had been dead quite some time. Some wore strange period clothing, while there were even some sitting in rags. The latter looked as though they were incredibly uncomfortable in their surroundings.

'Can I help you?' a snooty looking man across from me asked. He was dressed in a suit and looked as if he was used to being in charge, not sitting around waiting for someone else to tell him what to do.

'No, I'm sorry.' I stared at the ground, making a mental note not to make eye contact with any of the people in this place. I felt a sense of foreboding wash over me.

Eventually, I looked around the place once more, trying to distract myself from the awful thoughts that kept popping into my head. There was a coffee table in front of me, with a large glass vase containing white lilies. How very appropriate I thought, lilies for the dead. The only thing missing was a neatly arranged pile of magazines. I couldn't help but smile when I thought back to the day I had met Mary. My idea about a guide to the afterlife didn't seem so silly now. At least it would have filled the time and helped me to figure out some of the key points to this existence that I was obviously missing.

The time; when I thought about it, I realised that time seemed to be passing incredibly slowly. Considering it usually ran away from me, I could have sworn it was passing even slower than it would have on earth. I wondered if the feeling was caused by my surroundings, or whether it was purely the fear and dread that was knotted in my stomach making the moments drag like hours. Then I noticed the clock in the corner. There were no numbers displayed upon it, and it seemed to have too many hands, though it was ticking. The clicking noise reverberated around the space and it was definitely ticking much slower than a clock would on earth.

There were large glass windows along one side of the room, but it was so bright outside I couldn't make out any details of what lay beyond. It was like the sun was streaming in and I couldn't see anything other than its brightness. It should have been uncomfortable to look at, but for some strange reason it wasn't.

The place also felt warm, similar to when you step off an airplane on holiday and feel the warmth of the place hit you, seep into your bones. I hadn't felt warmth like this since I had been alive. Not even David's warmth was quite this, consuming. In a strange way, I felt as though the warmth was coming from my body rather than my surroundings.

I glanced at my hands, 'Nope,' I muttered. I had been hoping that I wouldn't be grey here. Silly, I thought. I had already been looking at the other dead people in the room. They were grey; why would I be any different.

Several moments passed and I could no longer hide from the nervous feeling that had been growing inside me. What if Mary was right about this whole thing, what if I was going to be punished? I could feel a great sense of confusion around me, but didn't know whether that was coming from within me, or from the other people sitting in this strange place. Did they feel the same way?

I started trying to think of what I could say to the powers that be when they came to get me. After all, despite my scheming, I hadn't ended up here deliberately. Surely that had to count for something.

'Susan...' I muttered and felt a stab of pain in my chest. I instinctively stared around the room as though I should be able to see her. She had to be here somewhere, surely. She had died, that was why the light came for us in the first place. Well, came for her, I was just a hitchhiker really.

Suddenly I heard muffled voices from behind the frosted glass and a man appeared in the doorway. He looked strange, not the same as me, or any of the other dead people sitting in the room. He wasn't grey at all. He seemed to glow, bright white and his blond beard looked like spun gold. He wore a modern business suit, except that it was completely white, matching his white shirt and tie.

'Portia?' he said, looking at me smiling. 'If you would be so kind as to step this way.'

I got to my feet and heard a woman sitting two seats from me mutter, 'Good luck.'

I glanced at her and smiled. She looked to be a kind lady in her mid forties and was sitting clutching a handbag in her lap, looking decidedly nervous.

The man gestured for me to enter Interview Room One, so I walked forward, not wanting to appear uncooperative.

'My name is Stanley. Please, take a seat,' he said, motioning to a chair as he sat back down behind a large desk. 'Let me have a quick look at your file.' He opened a white cardboard folder and began to leaf through the pages within.

I sat down, feeling rather sheepish. Somehow, this wasn't what I had expected from Heaven. While it was probably the most extraordinary place I had ever been to, it still had such a strange sense of banality to it. There was also something about this character, Stanley. I don't know why, but he appeared decidedly smug. His demeanour was perfectly suited to a bureaucrat.

'Well, well,' he said, crossing his hands and placing them on the desk in front of him. 'We have gotten into some mischief haven't we?'

'I'm sorry,' I muttered, my voice no more than a whisper. 'I didn't mean to end up here, it just sort of happened.'

'I understand,' he said, smiling. 'That's why we have this place. It's for people like you who need to be processed for return.'

'Return,' I mumbled. He made me sound like a parcel.

'Yes,' he continued, obviously used to giving this speech to confused people. 'Unfortunately it happens;

you get people who cross over by accident. This is usually caused by being too close to someone else as they cross over.'

'Susan...' I muttered once more.

'Yes,' he said, glancing at the file in front of him once more, his smile not masking the sense of boredom in his voice. 'Susan, your sister, yes?'

'Yes,' I replied. 'Where is she?'

'Not here, I'm afraid,' he said. 'This place is just for returns, as I said. I don't have the relevant information to tell you where she is at the moment. Unfortunately it takes some time for the paperwork to be updated, you understand.'

He was still smiling at me, and somehow this seemed to make me angry. Didn't we matter? We were the people forced to live down on earth, purely to keep the population levels under control for the chosen few who were selected to have a VIP afterlife.

'Something the matter, dear?' he asked, sensing my irritation.

'Yes,' I replied, sounding braver than I felt. 'I don't think this is quite right.'

'What do you mean?' he asked, pretending to root through my paperwork once more. 'Don't tell me you think you should stay?' His tone was now mocking and it only served to fuel the fire within me.

'I don't know that I do want to stay here,' I said, glancing around the place, hoping that my tone would suggest I was far from impressed, 'but that doesn't mean that you don't owe me some common courtesy.'

'I'm sorry,' he said, colour rising in his cheeks. He obviously wasn't used to someone answering back.

'Perhaps you don't fully appreciate what life is like down there,' I continued. 'I didn't ask to be sent here, but I think you should perhaps treat me with a little respect.'

'I see,' he replied angrily. 'I'm not accustomed to people such as *you* being quite so rude. You can't go blaming others, just because you didn't make the cut.'

'What exactly does that mean?' I asked. 'People such as me? I didn't make it into your snooty club due to a technicality. You're probably only here because you died early enough!'

'Really,' he said, his voice raised and his hands balling into fists.

'Is there a problem here?' A man's voice said from the doorway. I felt wary of the presence behind me; I hadn't even heard the door open.

'Yes,' Stanley replied. 'I think there is.'

'Stanley, perhaps you should step outside,' the newcomer said, sounding perfectly calm.

Stanley, obviously not amused, rose from his desk and stomped from the room. A new member of the god squad stepped forward and took his seat. I still felt angry, and I wasn't about to let Stanley's boss fob me off.

'My name is Nathan,' he said, smiling at me. 'What seems to be the problem, Portia?' He asked, not looking down at my file.

I was slightly taken aback that this person seemed to know who I was. Unlike Stanley, there was something completely gentle about Nathan. He didn't have a beard and his clean shaven face was boyish, offset by the deep tone of his voice. Like Stanley, he was wearing a crisp white suit. I don't know why, but he made me think of a posh public school type. There was something other worldly about him, but at the same time, he had a cheeky twinkle in his eye.

'I...' I stuttered for a moment. All of my previous anger seemed to have melted away.

'Stanley can be a bit of a forthright chap,' Nathan said, not needing to hear my explanation. 'We are simply here to make sure that you get to where you belong, and believe me Portia, you will be where you belong.'

'Of course,' I said, somehow unable to argue with this man, if that's what he was.

'You are unhappy with your life on earth?' he asked.

'No,' I replied.

'Jolly good,' he said, with an angelic smile.

'I didn't mean to end up here,' I continued.

'I see,' he said, looking down at my file for the first time. 'It says here that you are a known security risk. So you weren't actively trying to gain entry?'

'I thought about it,' I stuttered, feeling as though I had been caught doing something I oughtn't to be, 'but I didn't go through with it.'

'I see,' he said, smiling once more, 'but you have questions?'

'I guess,' I said, feeling confused. 'Is that allowed?'

'Of course,' he said. 'We at the Bureau for Earth Bound Relations are here to help ensure that those who live on the earthly plane have as happy an existence as possible.'

'Bureau...' I muttered.

'It's a lot to take in,' he continued. 'Please, let me know of anything I can clarify for you.'

'Why didn't I get in?' I blurted out.

'An obvious question,' he said, looking through the paperwork. 'You were destined for something else.'

'What?' I asked.

'I see you have a friend, David?' he asked.

'Yes,' I muttered, feeling a pang of guilt at the thought of David down on earth, frantic thinking that I had left him.

'You were meant for David,' he said matter-of-factly.

'So some of us stay for love?' I asked.

'Yes,' he said, smiling. 'We try not to be too cruel, especially to the guides.'

'Guides?' I asked, now thoroughly confused.

'Yes, guides,' he said, looking slightly bewildered. 'You don't know what a guide is?'

'Erm,' I said, wracking my brain.

'Really,' he said, tutting under his breath. 'I always said we should issue pamphlets, but the others think that would be overkill.'

'I could have done with one,' I replied, smiling slightly.

He sighed. 'There are those who are kept on earth in order to be guides, to help lost souls.'

'Ah,' I said. 'Yes, Mary is one of those.'

'Let me see,' he said, glancing at the pages before him. 'Yes, it says here that a lady, Mary, helped you when you first started out. She is a guide. We always ensure that guides get to be with their true love. Whether that be a love from their living lives, or the love they were destined for after death. It's only fair after all.'

'I don't understand,' I said, 'Mary is the guide, what does that have to do with me?'

'David is a guide,' he said, looking at me with a strange expression. 'You don't know this?'

'I don't think he does either,' I told him. This all sounded completely bizarre.

'Really?' he said. Well this is a case and point! We can't have guides wandering around with no bally idea what their vocation is… You say he doesn't know?'

'No,' I said. 'If you want some feedback, none of us know anything about anything. We blunder around trying to make the best of things, but there isn't a great deal of information to go on.'

'I see,' he said, 'this is very serious indeed.'

'What now?' I asked.

'Hmm…' he said, his mind deep in thought. 'Well,' he said eventually, 'we need to send you back.'

'Okay,' I uttered, still feeling somewhat unsatisfied. 'Can I ask one more thing?'

'Yes,' he said, his smile gone now. He was obviously eager to get back to his work, especially since I seemed to have brought the news that his well oiled machine wasn't working quite as well as he'd hoped.

'Why do you split up families?' I asked. It was David I was thinking of, and Beth and Mary. My family wasn't really an issue, but I knew it had hurt them to be separated from their living families. It seemed to be ruining Mr Weatherby's existence.

'Family isn't really an important concept in heaven,' he replied. 'We are all family here,' he continued. 'I suppose when we put the structure in place, we didn't consider it. It was purely down to quotas and lists. Is it a problem?'

'For some,' I said, feeling as though the life in Heaven must be more alien than I realised. 'Some of the souls I live with have been deeply hurt by losing those they love.'

'I see,' he said, 'I would say that we didn't realise that those who stayed on earth would still be bound by the ties they had in their living lives there.'

'They are,' I replied. 'I don't know how it feels to be in Heaven, but to live on earth without them is hard. One of my friends on earth, Mr Weatherby, lives his afterlife completely heartbroken.'

'You've given me a lot to think about,' he said. 'I think it's time we made some changes.'

'Such as?' I asked.

'Perhaps allow people to decide if they would prefer to stay with their families rather than being split up. It would mean more people on your end, obviously we couldn't open the gates here for families; it would be chaos.'

'Yes,' I muttered. 'It's a shame it's too late for the people I know.'

'Never say never,' Nathan said, winking at me.

I smiled, suddenly feeling strangely weary. I wanted to see my dead family again.

'Now,' he said, standing up from his desk, 'Let's get you home.'

'What do we do?' I asked.

'Why, what do you normally do,' he said, smiling and shaking his head. 'Think of home.'

'Is that it?' I asked, feeling slightly disappointed. 'I don't suppose that works the other way?'

He shook his head, 'No, indeed it does not.' His words sounded stern, but I could tell that he wanted to laugh. 'Now, off with you!'

'Thank you, Nathan,' I said.

'It's been a pleasure, Portia,' he answered, with a salute. 'I've always said we should conduct focus groups. Perhaps now the chaps in charge will listen to me!'

I laughed at the thought. 'Goodbye.'

'Goodbye, my young friend,' he said, as I faded from the room.

When I arrived back on earth, I was on the beach, right where I had been standing before the light had come. It didn't seem as though any time had passed at all. David was running along the sand. Just as I glanced back to where Susan lay on the ground in front of me, the man leaning over her jumped back while she spluttered, water spewing from her mouth; she opened her eyes.

'Susan!' I cried, feeling I might burst with joy.

'Portia…' she muttered.

'Don't try to speak,' the stranger said, lifting up her head. 'Nod if you can hear me.'

Susan nodded weakly and strained to try to sit up. She was staring in my direction and trying to lift a hand to shield her eyes.

'What's wrong?' the man asked.

'Nothing,' she said, flopping back down. 'I thought I saw someone.'

'Can you tell me your name?' The man asked.

'Susan Goldman,' she said, colour starting to come back into her cheeks, but only barely.

'Susan,' the man said wrapping his coat around her. 'We're going to get you to the hospital, is there someone we can phone for you?'

'Dad…' she muttered.

'Dad's on his way,' I said, hoping that the information would sink in.

She seemed to sigh, visibly relieved. I hadn't felt so close to my family for a long time, but something about our connection on the cold wet beach, meant that even if she couldn't hear my voice, she could feel me at least.

At that, David appeared at my side. 'What the hell were you playing at!' he yelled.

'David,' I said taking his face in my hands. 'I'm right here.'

'I saw you,' he said, his voice still angry. 'You were too damn close, Portia.'

'I wasn't just close, David, I was there,' I said, smiling at him.

'What do you mean?' he asked, bewildered. It was as though the smile on my face didn't fit the scene. 'I don't understand, Portia.'

'She's going to be okay,' I muttered, looking back at my sister.

'I'm glad,' he said, his expression strained, 'but what did you mean when you said, you were there?'

I didn't need to answer his question, he looked into my eyes and seemed to understand.

'So...' he mumbled. 'You're back?'

'I came home,' I replied, kissing him softly. 'I'll always come home.'

He took me into his arms.

'I think we should head back,' I said, glancing at Susan. 'Something tells me she's going to be okay. She fought for her life; I don't think she'll be so eager to throw it away again.'

Beth appeared at David's side; she looked ashen, even given our complexion.

'Don't worry,' I said, smiling at her. 'We need to go home, we have a lot to discuss.'

David looked puzzled, and still worried somehow. When I thought about it, I realised that everything I was saying must sound completely bizarre.

Prudence and Jonah had materialised behind us and looked on at the scene concerned.

'It's fine,' I said, smiling at the pair.

'Very good,' Jonah said, not looking wholly convinced.

'Take care,' Prudence said, with understanding. I wondered if she did understand.

'Come,' I said, squeezing David's hand and reaching out for Beth with the other.

Chapter Sixteen
A Welcome Visitor?

When we got back, David and Beth were both extremely anxious for me to tell them all that had happened, but I thought it was something I needed to share with the entire family. It affected all of us after all, with the little knowledge we had to go on; they deserved to know everything I had learned.

It didn't take too long to get the group gathered together, although Mr Weatherby was a bit stubborn. In the end, I had asked Mr Fibbers to go into his room and coax the old man downstairs.

Betsy grew restless as we waited for the old man, she had always been impatient with him hiding himself away. It was just her nature. In her own matronly way, she hated to see people unhappy.

Mary was the most fascinated. We hadn't actually told any of them what had happened on the beach, yet I could sense a great deal of curiosity emanating from her. Her gifts as a guide were obviously giving her a sense of what we were going to discuss, even if she didn't know the details.

Finally, they were all seated on the various sofas in the drawing room, even Mr Fibbers was watching me intently.

As the story unfolded I heard several gasps. Mr Weatherby tried to interrupt when I reached the part about his wife, but Mary touched his hand and motioned for him to be silent.

'What does this all mean?' the old man asked, once I had finally finished. There was desperation in his voice that I hadn't heard before. It had been difficult for him to sit in silence and listen to me talking.

'I don't really know,' I replied, shrugging my shoulders. 'I don't know whether they will be able to change things, but at least they know how things are down here for us. I would hope it at least means that what has happened to you won't happen to anyone else.'

'That's something,' Mary said, touching the old man's hand once more.

He didn't seem comforted by this thought. It was as though this new information had lit a spark inside him which had been dead for a long time. Dead even longer than he had been dead himself, hope. It had gone with his wife. I knew by looking into his newly intense eyes, that he would give anything to be with her again.

'What about me?' David asked.

I had seen him turn pale when I had recounted what Nathan had told me about his unknown gifts. Part of me felt guilty, perhaps it hadn't been fair to tell him that bit of information in front of everyone else. It would change so much of what he had understood his existence to be.

'Don't worry, David,' Mary said, smiling over at him. 'Being a *guide* is a great thing.'

He tried to smile at her, but I knew he was unnerved by the whole thing.

'It's strange that I understand more about it now,' she continued. 'Thank you, Portia.'

I smiled sheepishly. 'I didn't do anything…'

'You did,' Henry added. 'I knew I was meant to be with Mary, but now I realise it's more than that. Across the centuries, we were destined for one another. She's who I was born to be with.'

Mary glowed at his words and leaned her head on his shoulder.

'Yes,' I replied, crossing the room and sitting on the arm of the chair next to David. 'It means I was meant for you. From the moment I was born, this was always going to be my destiny.'

This seemed to make him happier and he put his hand on my knee. 'I'm going to need some help, Mary,' he said, glancing over at her. 'Why didn't I realise this before?'

She looked even more angelic than usual. 'Of course I'll help,' she beamed. 'I'll be happy to teach you everything I know, such as it is. Just think of the souls we'll be able to help working together. There's no need to worry about the past. It's partially my fault. I knew I could sense something more in you, but I didn't recognise that you were like me.'

The group no longer focussed upon me, were discussing different things about what my visit to other side could mean. I just sat and listened to them. They didn't seem to need any further contribution from me. David shifted along the couch and I slid down to sit next to him. As I did so, Mr Fibbers leapt from his position on the floor onto my lap and curled up into a ball. I could feel something powerful emanating from the little creature. It was a feeling of love. I think he loved me even more for giving his owner a new sense of purpose.

Then all of a sudden, a very strange thing happened.

A deep bell rang and the sound reverberated through the room. I don't know that any of us actually realised what it was at first. Silence descended and we looked around at one another in stunned silence.

'Was that…?' David's voice trailed off as Mr Fibbers leapt from my lap and meandered out into the hall.

Beth looked petrified, but at the same time she was the first one up out of her seat, following our feline friend out into the gloom.

Eventually we all followed the little cat as he confidently padded up to the front door. He then glanced around at us as though we were all total idiots. The little man always seemed to understand everything before we did. Even in death, a cat's senses were far superior to human ones.

'The bell?' Mr Weatherby said incredulously.

'It seems so,' Mary replied, equally flabbergasted.

Just then, the bell chimed again. As it did, we all froze once more, none of us sure exactly what this strange turn of events could mean.

'Should we invite them in?' I asked. I knew that we couldn't open the long locked up door, but if it was one of our kind, surely all they needed was an invitation.

'Certainly not!' Mr Weatherby exclaimed. 'Who knows what sort of lay-about could be trying to gain entrance. We don't want to be lumbered with some hideous creature as Portia was.'

'That's true,' Henry said, eyeing the door warily, as though he thought it might suddenly burst off it's hinges.

'David,' Mary said, 'take my hand.'

'What?' he asked, confused.

'Just do it,' she said, sighing.

He moved from my side and took her hand, looking slightly confused.

'This should be a good opportunity for you to use your abilities. I can guide you, we should easily be able to tell if the person on the other side of the door means us ill,' she said, closing her eyes.

David looked rather nervous, 'I don't really know what I'm doing,' he stuttered.

'Yes, you do,' she replied. 'You do it all the time, you just haven't realised it's what you're doing. Follow my lead.'

She closed her eyes once more and eventually David followed suit. The two of them stood there for several seconds before they opened their eyes once more. Mary looked intrigued.

'What?' Mr Weatherby asked, desperate to know who had found them at their home.

'I don't know,' Mary said, looking confused yet fascinated. 'It doesn't make a great deal of sense. I've never felt anything quite like it, but I know one thing...'

'They're not evil,' David finished, his face contorted as he tried to sense more from the being waiting outside.

'Are you going to let me in or not?' a male voice called from outside.

Beth appeared at David's side and he put an arm around her to reassure her.

'I'm still not sure,' Mr Weatherby said, backing away a little.

Mr Fibbers shook his head. I got the impression that if he could speak he would have been muttering some sarcastic jibe.

'I trust Mary,' Henry stated. 'If she says this person means us no harm, then I say we let him in.'

'Fine,' Mr Weatherby spat. 'I don't know why I opened my home to you lot, I don't get a say in anything these days.'

Mary took the old man's griping as agreement and cleared her throat. 'Come in,' she said, clearly and loudly.

'Finally,' the man remarked, materialising in front of us.

'Nathan?' I uttered, completely taken aback. Even earthbound, this strange man didn't look at all dead. He emitted a light that filled the darkened hallway as though the sun were streaming in.

'Really,' he continued, ignoring my confusion. 'I know we gave you the ability to protect your homes, but I didn't realise you would be so suspicious!'

'I'm sorry,' I said, feeling I should be the one to speak. 'You never know who's skulking about down here. Everyone, this is Nathan, he's the er… gentleman I told you about.'

'Ah,' Nathan said, smiling. 'I see I need no introductions.'

The group didn't answer; they just all stood there dumb-struck.

'Well,' he said after several moments, 'shall we?'

I realised he was looking for us to continue the conversation somewhere more suitable, so I led the group towards the living room.

Once we were all gathered, Nathan took a seat by the fire, facing the group and took his time looking at each of us in turn.

Mr Fibbers leapt up onto the newcomer's lap and was padding around on his knee, trying to find somewhere comfortable to settle down.

This seemed to shock the visitor and David and I had to stifle a laugh as the man struggled to comprehend what the little creature was doing.

'I think he likes you,' I said, smiling.

'I see,' Nathan replied. 'I suppose that's something. I've never actually come across one of these before.'

'It's a cat,' I said, puzzled by the man's answer. If he had lived on earth, surely he had seen a cat before.

'Right,' he said, nodding. 'I've heard of those. Forgive me, it's my first time down here.'

This seemed to puzzle everyone; who was this strange being sitting before us?

'What are you?' Betsy asked. She wasn't being rude, it was obvious that she was just bursting with curiosity.

'Well…' he stuttered. 'I'm a representative from The Bureau for Earth Bound Relations.' I think he thought that this would be enough of an answer to explain Betsy's question.

She smiled and nodded in response but it was obvious that this hadn't been exactly what she had meant.

'Perhaps I should tell you why I'm here,' he continued, trying to bring the meeting to order.

'That would be helpful,' Mr Weatherby said. Even though everyone was awestruck by this strange being, it didn't mean that the old man would be any more courteous to him than he was to anyone else.

'Yes,' Nathan replied. He wasn't used to someone addressing him in that manner, obviously. 'Well, it's quite simple. I take it that Portia has filled you in on what happened during her visit *upstairs*?'

The group nodded and muttered that they did.

'Well, after a very long and tedious feasibility study, I was able to convince the others at the Bureau that what Portia had to say held some merit.'

'Long and tedious?' I asked.

'Ah, well...' he muttered. 'Time not really passing the same way, and all that...'

'Get to the point,' Mr Weatherby cut in. It was strange. Nathan seemed to command a presence that made people feel calm and open, but something had taken hold of Mr Weatherby that couldn't be controlled.

'Yes,' Nathan continued, not used to this sort of reaction, 'as I was saying... I managed to convince them that perhaps there wasn't the right amount of choice given to those who were allocated to stay on the earthly plane. Also, that perhaps the guides should be given a certain amount of training upon arrival etc...'

'I see,' I said, smiling. I couldn't believe what I was hearing. 'So what are they, I mean, you, going to do about it?'

'Make some changes,' Nathan said, clapping his hands together. Mr Fibbers jumped at the noise and leapt from his lap. 'Ah, sorry about that, little chap.'

'He'll be fine,' I said, as Mr Fibbers padded over and jumped onto my lap, shooting Nathan a derisive glance.

'So, first order of business!' Nathan continued. 'Loved ones torn asunder and all that... We have decided to have a little test run at giving people a choice to be together. As I mentioned, it's not feasible for us to take a whole new tranche of people into heaven, but I think we could start a campaign in heaven to allow those who wish to do so, to return to earth to be with those they left behind.'

'How long would that take?' Mr Weatherby asked.

'Not long in your terms,' Nathan said, smiling. 'Although Portia did make me aware of your case, ah, Mr Weatherby, isn't it?

'Yes,' he replied, his voice now no more than a whisper, all his shortness completely gone.

'We decided to treat you as a test case. Your loved one was contacted and as it turns out, she is more than happy to return here to be with you.'

'Really?' the old man gasped. I don't think he dared believe it was true.

'Yes,' Nathan replied.

'What about us?' Beth asked in tiny whisper. 'Can we have our mum and dad back?'

'That's a more complicated one I'm afraid,' Nathan said. 'It is on the agenda for the next quarter, but there are still those who feel that guides should still reside here without their living families. It's believed it would be too much of a distraction for them.'

I could see that both Mary and David were rattled by Nathan's words.

'I'm not saying I agree,' Nathan said, holding his hands up, 'but you have to understand, the rules have been in place for such a long time, it's not always easy to get people to change their way of thinking. I'm sure, if this first step is a success, it should lead the way for more changes in the future. You never know, it may also free up some space in Heaven, depending upon the number of people who chose to return. In fact, I think it was that fact that finally swayed the others.'

'It's not very fair,' David said, knowing his sister wasn't likely to have the courage to say anything more. 'Beth isn't a guide, why should she suffer? In fact, if guides aren't allowed to be with their living families, why are we together in the first place?'

Nathan clicked his fingers and a file appeared in his hands. He leafed through it for several seconds. 'As I thought...' he mused.

'What?' David asked, curious as to whose file the man was perusing.

'Well,' Nathan started, trying to choose his words carefully. 'While I'm sure there will be others in a similar situation to your sister who didn't have a choice, I'm afraid she did...'

'What choice?' Beth asked, her voice almost inaudible.

'You could have crossed over,' Nathan replied. 'It would appear that you chose to remain here.'

'To be with me!' David exclaimed. 'Yet again, it's not her fault that I have to be here.'

'I'm sorry,' Nathan said, 'but your sister chose such a sacrifice. If you would like, I could probably have her admitted up there? After a suitable appeal process of course...'

'What?' Beth stuttered. 'No... I don't want to leave you...' she was looking at her brother pleadingly. She was always frightened by change, and this new information seemed to deeply unsettle her.

'Don't worry,' he said. 'No one is going to make you do anything you don't want to do.'

'As you wish,' Nathan said. 'Not meaning to sound short, but I think we should get on with things.'

'What do I need to do?' Mr Weatherby asked, assuming that Nathan was referring to himself and his wife.

'Nothing,' Nathan replied. 'Once we are finished here, I will deliver your wife to you.'

It was all Mr Weatherby could do to sit still. He looked elated, but at the same time very nervous. I noticed that he reached up and touched his hair, as though he was now suddenly anxious about his appearance.

'What is there still to discuss?' Mary asked.

'The training,' Nathan said, sighing. 'If you will agree, I would like you and David to come with me. I need to give you some guidance, find out what you know and what you don't, that kind of thing.'

Henry reached across and took Mary's hand, obviously not happy at the thought of her leaving.

'I will, of course, return you here once we are finished,' Nathan qualified. 'In fact, given the way time works here, I'm sure it won't feel like any time at all.'

Mary looked at David. 'What do you think?'

He hesitated for several moments. It was clear that his previous exchange with Nathan had made him wary of the heavenly being. 'I'm happy to go if you are,' he replied eventually.

'Well then,' Nathan said, 'let's get this done, shall we?'

He rose from his chair and held his hands out for David and Mary to take hold of.

As they each walked over and took the hold of one of the stranger's hands, the man looked at me and smiled. 'Thank you, Portia. You don't know how much you have done.'

I didn't know what to say. When he smiled at you like that, it was hard to focus; so I just smiled sheepishly and nodded my head.

With that, they were gone. As the room darkened with Nathan's absence, I felt a strange cold sensation wash over me. It was the lack of David in my world. Beth and Henry seemed to be feeling the same thing, and without words, we huddled together and held one another for reassurance.

I hoped that Nathan was right, and that very soon the three of us would have our loved ones back with us.

We should have trusted Nathan, it felt as though mere seconds had passed when an all encompassing light filled the room and David and Mary returned to our world. The light engulfed the space completely. Totally blinding, somehow I knew it was them. I could sense David's presence before I could see him.

I don't understand why we were all so shocked, but as they returned, we noticed they had a middle aged woman with them. She had sparkling bright green eyes and fair hair which was faded to grey in places, although this wasn't easy to spot given our deathly pallor. Her exquisite emerald green gown brought out the colour in her eyes all the more.

'Eleanor,' Mr Weatherby muttered, his eyes glistening with tears.

His wife obviously had more confidence than he, who was in shock. She ran across the space between them and took her husband into her arms.

'I've missed you, Theo,' she said, taking a step back to look at his face.

What happened next took us all completely by surprise.

'What the...' David said, voicing what we were all thinking.

In the instant that Mr Weatherby had touched his wife, his entire appearance changed. He still looked like the same man, but it was as though he was ten years younger, more perhaps. Gone were the jowls around his face and the stern appearance of his eyes. Even his clothes had changed into a dashing grey suit with a bright blue silk waistcoat.

'She's brought him to life,' Betsy said, her eyes glistening.

'That's love for you,' Mary said, striding over to Henry and folding herself into his arms.

David walked over to Beth and me and took us into an embrace. 'I've missed you,' he muttered, 'both of you.'

'It wasn't so long,' I said, smiling.

'Maybe for you,' he replied.

'You have to tell us everything,' Beth said, her face alive with wonder.

'Later,' David uttered, stroking his sister's hair. 'We have all the time in the world.'

Beth sighed, but seemed happy enough. I think we both were. It had been extremely disconcerting not having him around. 'Where to now?' she asked.

'I think I know just the place,' David said, smiling.

'Are we going outside?' she asked, warily.

'Take a deep breath,' I said, smiling at her.

Instead she just closed her eyes and seemed to grit her teeth.

I should have known where we would end up, the park, the place where we had met.

'Is this?' Beth said, looking around.

'Yes,' David said smiling. 'It's the park near home. I thought you might like to see it again.'

Despite her earlier misgivings, it wasn't long before she was skipping along the path and trying to pick daisies. I knew she wasn't overly keen on the number of humans around the place, but she was definitely enjoying herself.

'So,' I said, sitting on the bench and gesturing for David to join me. It had been the place we had been when he had kissed me for the first time.

'So...'

'You a super hero guide now?' I asked, smirking.

He looked confused.

'Never mind,' I muttered.

'I just wanted to sit here with you again,' he said, looking around the place. 'I realised a few things on my visit with Nathan.'

'Oh?' I asked, unsure what this new revelation could be.

'Nothing really,' he said, 'I think it just helped me be more honest about what happened that first day I saw you here.'

'What?' I asked, totally confused.

'It was my gift,' he said, taking my hand and playfully stroking my fingers. 'I sensed you here and that's why I materialised. I hadn't actually felt a draw like that before.'

'So you sensed a lost soul…' I muttered looking out over the park.

'No,' he said laughing.

I looked round at him, he was grinning widely.

'I sensed you,' he said, touching my cheek. 'I think my overactive senses were trying to tell me you were the one I was supposed to find. Looking back, I don't know how I can have missed it.'

I laughed. 'Did you mention it to Nathan?'

He looked confused.

'I'm just thinking,' I continued, 'that since we all seem to be so clueless here, maybe there should have been a flashing neon sign above my head.'

He still looked confused.

'Never mind,' I said, smiling.

He reached in and kissed me, slow but intense, it made my head spin.

As he moved back, I gazed deep into his deep blue eyes.

In that moment, my world seemed to make perfect sense. Home wasn't a place; home was these guys. David, Beth, Mary, Betsy, Henry… even Mr Weatherby and his long lost wife. David was right, we had all the time in the world, and I couldn't wait to get started.

An Epilogue Of Sorts...

This new chapter of my life was something very unexpected. I couldn't tell you now how long had passed since our heavenly visitor had been among us. In some ways it could have been years, but in others, everything around us still felt new, so I knew it couldn't have been too long.

I had never felt more at peace, alive or dead. The only time I was ever restless, was when David was away on *assignment* with Mary, as he called it.

Mrs Weatherby seemed to have brought a new life to the place, and Mr Weatherby was a completely different person. He laughed and joked, and had even taken to playing Henry at chess.

Mr Fibbers seemed to spend all his time with David, Beth and me. Although, when we weren't all in a group, he didn't leave Beth's side.

'Why does he do that?' I commented one afternoon. I was sitting on a sofa in the library with my legs across David's lap, while Beth sat over by the fireplace stroking the feline upon her knee and humming mindlessly.

'Mr Weatherby doesn't need him anymore,' David said with certainty. 'Who knows, maybe the little creature is just following feline whims, but it I doubt it. I think that Beth needs him now, the same way you needed him when he first came into your life. Mr Fibbers is a guide all of his own.'

'You can sense that?' I asked.

'I can sense a lot of things these days,' he said, smiling.

I rolled my eyes.

'Yes, even that,' he said, pretending to clip me around the ear.

'You know I'm joking,' I said, reaching over to kiss his cheek.

'I know,' he said, taking my chin and turning his head, so he could kiss my lips.

'She is happy isn't she?' I asked, thinking on his words more seriously.

'Beth?' he asked.

'Yes,' I replied, watching her carefully. She looked content, but Mr Fibbers could obviously sense something we couldn't.

'She's fine,' David said, shrugging his shoulders. 'I think she'll just need a little reassurance for a while. She'll be off on adventures of her own before you know it.'

'Ahem,' Mr Weatherby said, appearing beside us, his wife standing behind him. 'David, would you mind giving us a couple of moments?'

'Of course,' David said, bemused. He disappeared from the sofa and reappeared in the armchair across from Beth.

Mr Weatherby sat down and his wife rested on the arm of the sofa, her hand placed lovingly upon her husband's shoulder. The old man seemed to be contemplating what he wanted to say.

As he did, I could see David in the corner, glancing over periodically. He never liked to be left out of anything. Even if he did try to act like a zen master these days, he was still the same old David underneath it all, guide or no guide.

'So, Portia,' Mr Weatherby began awkwardly.

'It's okay, Mr Weatherby,' I said, reassuringly. I had no idea what the old man wanted to say, but I wanted to put him at ease.

'Please,' he continued, embarrassed, 'call me Theodore.'

'Of course,' I stuttered, now the embarrassed one. 'Go on, Theodore.'

'First of all, I should have spoken to your sooner. I know that when you came to us, I was… less than welcoming, shall we say?'

'I understand,' I muttered.

'That's not the point,' he interrupted. 'I was a very sad person at that point in my life, or death should I say.'

I giggled and he looked confused. 'Sorry,' I uttered, 'that just sounded like something Mary might say.'

'Right,' he said, smiling. 'I just want you to know how grateful I am that you came here.'

'How grateful we both are,' his wife said, in her sing song voice.

'Anyway,' he said, 'I just wanted to thank you.'

'You're welcome,' I stuttered.

I smiled at him and for what felt like the first time since my arrival, he returned my smile before he and his wife faded from the room.

David materialised instantly at my side. 'What was that about?' he asked.

'Nothing,' I replied. 'He's just happy now.'

'Yes,' David said, taking my hand. 'I'm glad. I wouldn't be without you.'

'Nor me,' I replied kissing him once more. 'I love you, David; even if you do annoy the hell out of me sometimes.'

'Hey!' he replied. 'It's not my fault you're a simpleton. Your lack of brain power means you have a ridiculously short temper.'

I gave him a nudge and we both ended up laughing.

Beth appeared beside me, Mr Fibbers following at her heels. 'So what now?'

'Now,' I said, thoughtfully, glancing around the room at my family, 'now is forever…'

THE END

Clare Wilson

From Hamilton in Lanarkshire, Clare has a History degree from Strathclyde University and now lives in London with her husband. Having spent some time trying to find some magic in various fields, she is now concentrating on her career as a writer.

Clare was drawn to writing by her life long passion for reading and inventing stories. As a child, Clare loved nothing more than curling up on a window seat in her local library and being carried away by a magical story. A fantasy fiction fanatic, she has published two books in The Staff Wielder Series as well as writing other stories of a fantastical nature.

Other Books By Clare Wilson...

Book One in the Staff Wielder Series - The Long Staff

Book Two in the Staff Wielder Series - The Ancient Exile

Printed in Great Britain
by Amazon